Pressured

by SANTESHA V. PATTERSON

RoseDog 🐾 Books
PITTSBURGH, PENNSYLVANIA 15238

RoseDog Books
585 Alpha Drive
Suite 103
Pittsburgh, PA 15238
Visit our website at *www.rosedogbookstore.com*

ISBN: 978-1-4809-8139-3
eISBN: 978-1-4809-8116-4

CHAPTER 1

The day was May 14, 1980, that my whole life would change. My family and I lived in Texas at the time. I was fourteen years old at the time and was the youngest out of the three of us. My two older sisters, Darlene (fifteen) and Summer (seventeen), were always treating me bad because I was Dad's favorite. Often they pulled my hair and did everything else bullies would do. We were on our way back from the biggest fair ever and I don't know why Dad ended the trip so early but we really didn't pay it any mind. Once we headed back home he began acting so strange that we felt like we didn't know him anymore. Once Dad raised his voice the whole household would remain silent. As we pulled up in front of the house we owned my father hesitated to get out the car.

> Yona- What's wrong, Dan?
> Danny- Nothing, just get the kids upstairs and into the house.
> Yona- Are you sure you're okay, honey?
> Danny- Yona, just get the kids upstairs and into the house. Come on.
> As we all got out the car and walked up the stairs to the front door, Terrance, a good friend of mine that lived next door, came from out his house and ran over toward us.
> Terrance- Hey, Dan, can Black come outside to play with me?
> Danny- No, not right now, she has a couple of chores to do around

the house. Maybe later.

Terrance- Well, there….

Danny- No, I don't want to hear it. I said later.

Black- Please, Dad?

Danny- No. Open the door, Yona.

My sisters began to laugh. My mother stuck the key in the door and we followed in behind her. My dad looked around the side of the house before he came inside and closed the door. As soon as my mother turned on the light three men stood in the living room with guns pointing them at us. My heart jumped, as my mother and sisters stood there petrified. We had no idea what was going on.

Danny- What are you doing here, Zane?

Zane- You know why I'm here, Danny. Stop acting stupid. Are you going to give me the codes or do I have to murder your whole family?

Danny- I told you once and I'll tell you again, no.

Just then Zane pointed the gun at my oldest sister, Summer, and shot her twice in the chest. My sister fell lifeless to the floor. My mother began screaming and ran for Zane but he shot her twice also. My mother fell backwards and died immediately. I began crying as my father stared in a daze. I couldn't believe it. This man just killed my oldest sister and mother and he did it for no reason. What the hell was going on? Why was it that my dad knew this man and we never saw him before?

Zane- That's two down, Dan, what's it going to be?

Danny- You mother fucker, I'm going to kill you when I get my hands on you. You can't have the codes because the codes don't belong to you. You'll never get them, ever, you hear me?

Zane- Yeah, I hear you but now hear me.

Zane turned and pointed the gun at my sister Darlene and fired one shot at her head. As my sister fell to the floor my body clamped up. I just knew he was going to kill me. My father cried as if he was a baby. That only left the two of us alone. He looked at me with tears in his eyes.

Danny- I'm sorry, baby. I love you. You were always Daddy's favorite.

Zane had no sympathy for my dad whatsoever. He pointed the gun at him and smiled.

Zane- Alright, Danny boy, are you going to give me the codes or what?

Danny- No. See you in hell, mother fucker. (He closed his eyes.)

Zane- Have it your way.

Zane fired the last two rounds into my father's skull. I screamed until I couldn't scream anymore. I felt weak and mistreated as Zane walked over toward me.

Black- He's not going to kill me, he's not going to kill me.

Zane- How do you know I'm not going to kill you?

Black- You don't have any more rounds.

Zane- (shocked) Well, I see you know your guns. What else do you know? Do you have a boyfriend?

Black- No.

Zane- No. Well, do you like boys?

Black- Yes, but I have no business with them.

Zane- That's smart, who taught you that?

Black- My mother did.

Zane- Your mother, huh? Well, your mother is dead and she doesn't know shit. Did she ever tell you about sex? Did she?

Black- No.

Zane- Well, I'll teach you.

Just then Zane pushed me down on the floor and began raping me. He ripped off my shirt as if it were an old piece of cloth. I began screaming at the top of my lungs for him to stop but he wouldn't. Just then the other two men ran over and took my jeans off as Zane held my arms down. I tried to hold them onto me with the strength of my legs but I wasn't strong enough. As one of the men threw my pants in the corner the other ripped off my panties. I could hear Zane unbutton, then unzip his pants. I really began to panic. Then it happened. I screamed as Zane shoved his penis in me with extreme force. I've never experienced such pain in my life. I don't know what came over me but I gave in. I just lay there because I would rather be raped than dead. When he was finished he whipped the sweat from his face with a handkerchief, then threw it at me.

Zane- Clean yourself up.

I was expecting him to shoot me but instead he just walked away with the other two men behind him, then they closed the door. Once I heard a car start and pull off I began screaming and crying at the top of my lungs. Just when I thought no one heard me Terrance came through the door. He went into total shock once he saw my family dead and me lying naked on the floor.

Black- Terrance, please, I need some help.
Terrance- I tried to tell your dad that those men were inside your house but he didn't want to hear it. (He grabbed a blanket off the chair, then put it on me.) Come on, Black, you got to make it. Ma, help!

Ten years later....

Who'd ever have thought I'd make it to twenty-four? I know I sure didn't. The police tried to find the man who murdered my family but it was useless. He vanished and they couldn't find him since that day. I know he was on this planet somewhere just watching me. I just knew it. What did he want? Ever since that little incident fourteen years ago I haven't trusted anyone since, especially men. I hardly talked to them. The only man I trusted in this lifetime was Terrance. He was twenty-four also and very handsome, might I say. His mother, Judy, took me in once they couldn't find any of my family. The ones that they did find didn't want me. When I turned sixteen we moved from Texas to Manhattan. Judy thought it would be a better atmosphere for Terrance and me. Few things pleased me. In fact, nothing pleased me but that dress in the window on 125th Street. I would look at that dress every day of the week except for when the store was closed. I would park my jeep and walk three blocks just for the fun of it. The cost for the dress was five thousand dollars. Yes, I know that's a little ridiculous for a dress but it was something special about that dress. It meant a sign of freedom. I had received my father's savings once I reached twenty-one so Judy and I moved in a mansion. Terrance moved on his own, to Brooklyn, though he often visited. I was saving my money to get my life straight. I know you're wondering what in my life do I have to get straight but I'll get to that a little later in the story. Suddenly, my thoughts were interrupted.

Thomas- Black, I need to speak with you.

I turned around to find that it was Thomas, my boss. He scared the hell out of me. In fact, he always scared me. I smiled at him as he smiled back.

Thomas- Come on, get in the limo. I have to talk to you.

As I walked over to the car Thomas opened the door from the inside for me. I got inside and closed the door. As I became comfortable I realized my group was in the car.

Black- What's up, Thomas?
Thomas- Alright. The new job you're going to do is Mr. Mann. The only bad thing is I'm going to have to take the men group off because they just went on vacation.
Black- What do you mean?
Grey- How are we....
Thomas- Yes, I know that you ladies have never been on the job alone but you're going to have to get used to it. The men aren't going to be here for a long time. Everything will be just fine.

When I turned eighteen I took an oath to be a professional thief. I was hoping to run into the man that murdered my family. We, as in me and four other women—Grey, Blue, Pink, and Red—rob big rich people and bring the goods to Thomas. He pays us each $5,000 for each job. I'm responsible for getting my girls in and out to safety in each job. I make decisions before anyone takes any big actions. Mr. Mann was a big-time drug dealer. His business was very known and popular. I felt unsure about doing a job without men, especially being that Mr. Mann was very dangerous when it came to his money. God only knew how many men he had guarding his club. Thomas wanted us to rob him and if that meant kill, then so be it. I knew I was capable of pulling the job, but were the others?

> Black- Are you guys ready for something like this? Do you think we can pull this job alone?
> Red- I'm ready.
> Blue- I am.
> Grey- I'm ready without a doubt.
> Pink- I'm not. I'm scared, Thomas.
> Thomas- (looking at Pink hard) What are you scared of?
> Black- Maybe she....
> Thomas- Shut up, Black. She can answer for herself.
> Thomas- Are you a little pussy? I mean, you do have one but are you?
> Pink- I'm just....
> Thomas- (putting his cane to Pink's neck) Look, don't fuck with me, do you got it?

Pink was soft hearted and that was a good and bad thing. She let her feelings get involved with her job. The last thing you needed was a heart when it came to this job. I felt sorry for her because even though she was 5'8", one hundred and seventy pounds with a pretty face and figure, she was trampled with issues. I always wondered would she survive in the real world, even though they say beauty gets you a long way, does it?

Thomas- You have to grow up, girl, you're twenty-two. Gain some heart for Christ. Be a woman. (He removed the cane from Pink's neck.)
Pink- I'm ready.
Black- Are you sure? A minute ago you weren't....
Thomas- (interrupting) She's ready.
Black- Alright, then she's ready.
Thomas- (throwing his hands up) Well, let's do this.

Deep down inside I knew Pink wasn't ready, but by Thomas' abuse she really had no choice. I talked to the girls for a while about what we were going to do then I walked back to my car. Blue decided she would walk with me. It was still early as Blue and I walked around the park before I went to get my car. Children were playing, laughing, dancing, and singing. It kind of made me wish I were a child again. The delicious smell of barbecue chicken polluted the air as we walked through. It was so beautiful that it was to die for. Looking at all of these children had me anxious to get home to Lily. She was not my legal child but I took care of her like she was. I moved her to the city when she was one and a half because of her hard knock life.

Blue- Looking at all of these kids makes me want to be a kid again.
Black- I was just thinking the same thing. Well, you know if we close our eyes and believe we can achieve.
Blue- (pushing Black) You know who you sound like, right?
Black- I know, that's why I said it. One day I'm going to push that man out of his wheelchair.
Blue- He doesn't have one.
Black- I know, when he gets one.
Blue- (laughing) You're stupid. (She let her laugh die down.) How's Lily?
Black- She's fine.
Blue- Recovering from that little accident well?
Black- She hardly talks about it. I don't think she remembers because

she was a baby.

Blue- Memories travel a long way, but hopefully it will skip her or someone will have to deal with an angry child.

Just then a German Shepard that jumped up into the air to catch a Frisbee landed on Blue's new peacoat and knocked her down to the ground.

Oh my god. (standing up dusting herself off) My husband is going to kill me. Thanks stupid mutt.

Black- You'll be alright, it's only a stain. You can take it to the cleaners.

Blue- Try to explain that to him. He's not going to want to hear it. Damn.

Black- You'll be okay.

I don't know why Blue was so uptight about her clothes. Ever since she married Felix she changed a lot. She's become more paranoid. Growing up with Blue I never thought that we would be this close. I was so used to Pink and Red until men came between us. I really didn't care because when it was time for business it was business.

Blue- What time is it?

Black- (looking at her watch) 4:23 P.M.

Blue- Shit, I have to get home, call me later. (She ran.) Don't forget.

Black- I won't. You sure you don't want a ride?

Blue- (still running) No.

I watched Blue run until she was out of sight, then I headed for my car. As I walked inside my house Lily greeted me at the door.

Lily- (giving Black a hug) Hi, Mommy. Are you here to stay?

Black- (hugging Lily) Yes, I am.

Lily- Mommy, guess who's here?

Black- (kissing Lily) Who, honey?

Lily- Terrance. You know, the one you like.

Black- (covering Lily's mouth) Now honey, be nice.

I was so happy Terrance came over. I enjoyed looking at that gorgeous man. Could it be because he saved my life or because he just was that attractive? I was not really scared of him, I just didn't know anything about men. So being turned on by him was like a new experience for me. If I knew about men the way I knew about guns then there would be no problem. As I came back to reality I noticed Terrance was walking right toward me. Maybe I thought out too loud.

> Terrance- What's up, girl? (He kissed Black on the cheek.)
> Black- (smiling) Nothing, just about to relax.

I wouldn't dare let another man kiss me the way that he did. He had that permission. Terrance made me feel very comfortable when he was around. I wasn't afraid of him. Suddenly I smelled something cooking in the kitchen. I knew exactly what it was.

> Terrance- Something smells good. What are you cooking, Judy? (He walked into the kitchen.)
> Terrance- (walking behind Black) It smells like your favorite.
> Judy- (smiling with her hands out, waiting for Black to enter the kitchen) Spaghetti and meatballs with garlic bread. (She gave Black a hug.) Hi, how was your day?
> Black- Fine. You're acting like you haven't seen me in years. I just left you this morning.
> Judy- Well, I was lonely all day until Terrance came over. He's staying for dinner.
> Black- Well, didn't Lily keep you company?
> Judy- Actually she stayed in her room all day today. She only came down once she heard Terrance. She was drawing Mickey and Minnie Mouse.

Terrance walked into the kitchen holding Lily. I enjoyed every minute of it. I wished that we really were a family because we looked cute together. I knew that Lily could never have her family back so we created a new one for her.

Lily- Mommy, can I help you set up the table? We can make it look so pretty for Terrance.

Black- (smiling) Sure, honey.

As Terrance watched television Lily and I set up the table while Judy continued to cook. After a while everything was all set up. The table encountered foods that could have resumed inside of cooking magazines.

Terrance- (smelling the food) I love when I come over to eat. Sometimes I want to come home just for a decent meal.

Candance- Well, if you came over more you wouldn't have that problem. (She dug in her blouse shirt pocket, pulling out a key.) Black, look at the lovely key Terrance made for me. It even has my initials carved in it.

Black- It's nice, I like it. (She looked at Terrance.)

I wished that he would come over more also. I enjoyed his company. The way he lifted his eyebrows when thinking was innocent.

Terrance- Isn't that right, Black?

Black- (leaving her thoughts, then answering) Sure.

Terrance- Well, you said that like you wanted me to leave.

Black- I'm sorry, I was just in thought. Of course we would love to have you over more often.

Lily- The food tastes good. Go Nanny, go Nanny.

Everyone felt like that was a cute moment so we laughed. Terrance rubbed her head to let her know that was cute, then began eating. The room grew quite as everyone ate. Terrance decided that he would give everyone the good news now.

Terrance- (clearing his throat) I have some great news for everyone.

I think you might like it.

Judy- (wiping her mouth with a napkin) What is it? (She put the key back in her blouse pocket.)

Lily- Can I stay here or do I have to go in another room?

Terrance- No, you don't have to go in another room. Well, being that I have been all around this world and back I find myself in the craziest predicaments. I'm deciding to....

Judy- To what?

Terrance- I've decided to get married and move to Atlantic City.

Lily- Wow, can I come with you?

Terrance- You can visit anytime you want.

Judy- That's good. I'm happy for you. Well, what's her name?

Terrance- Samantha.

Judy- When's the wedding?

Terrance- November 14.

Lily- Oh, can I be your flower girl?

Terrance- You're just the person I wanted to do the job.

Lily ran from her seat to Terrance and jumped on his lap, then gave him an enormous hug. I was upset. I could not believe that this man I loved was getting married on me. Whoever this woman was I know I would hate her and no way did I want to meet her.

Lily- Mommy, are you happy for Terrance?

Black- (disappointed but smiling) Yes, I am happy for him. In fact, I would love to sit in the front row and watch.

Lily- Can she sit in the front seat, Terrance?

Terrance- She sure can. (He avoided looking at Black.)

I wanted to smack him. Why, though? I wasn't in a relationship with him. I wanted to be but I wasn't. I was jealous completely. In fact, I wasn't even hungry anymore. Terrance could not even look at me because he knew I was hurt. Who wouldn't be?

Black- (standing up) Excuse me, I'm tired.

Judy- Black, you didn't even finish your food.

Black- Could you put it up for me? Thanks.

As I reached the top of the stairs I felt tears pushing through my eyes. Once I reached my room and closed the door I just let them go. How could he do this to me?

CHAPTER 2

The following morning I couldn't help but to just lie in bed due to the wonderful news Terrance had given us. I was so mad I had to fall asleep. That was my remedy to calming down. The sun shined so heavily in my face that I had to put my hand up to block it. I got up once I felt hunger pains in my stomach. I didn't even have a steady stomach to eat last night. Damn, I was jealous. Why did he have to go out and find someone else when I wanted to be that someone? I just didn't know what to do with a man as a woman. I didn't even care to know this woman because she already crossed the line with me, she just didn't know it. I decided to take a hot shower and go to Lews. That was the best place to have breakfast in any state. I knew by the time I got back Lily would be up and also hungry. After I got dressed I walked down the stairs and found a letter attached on the front door. It read: "If you're going to Lews bring me something back." I smiled, and took the note down because that woman knew me like the back of her own hand. On my way back from Lews in my way to the door I heard the phone ringing, so I hurried and opened the door.

Black- (running answering the phone) Hello?
Red- Hey, girl, what you doing?
Black- Nothing, just came back from Lews.
Red- I was going to go there but I changed my mind. I want to go to

that new clothing outlet that just opened up. We need something to wear for tonight.

Black- Girl, I almost forgot about that job we have tonight. I hope everyone's prepared because the last thing I need on my hands is a dead body.

Red- Well, the only person who I'm worried about is Pink. She better get it together.

Black- She sure enough better. Why did Thomas make us have to go on this job by ourselves anyway? This is new to all of us. I'm so used to the men. They're probably going to be away for the whole summer.

Just then Judy and Lily walked downstairs and noticed I left the front door open.

Judy- Well, I see we have animals living with us.

Lily- I think Mommy left it open.

Judy- (closing the door) I know. Did you get the food?

Black- It's on the table. Lily, you can sit at the table and eat.

Lily- Alright, thank you, Mommy.

Judy went over to the table and took out her and Lily's food.

Red- Tell everyone I said good morning.

Black- Havoc said good morning, everyone.

Judy- Who's Havoc?

Black- Red. (She laughed.)

Judy- Lord, you young ladies need to stop using these street names. You all need Jesus in your life.

Black- (laughing) You heard her.

Red- (laughing) Yeah.

Black- Where's Grey?

Red- Washing that funky tail.

Black- Well, when she gets dressed come and get me so we can get something to wear tonight.

Red- Okay. I'm going to call Pink and Blue, too.

Black- Alright, talk to you later.

We hung the phone up and I went to retrieve my hot breakfast. As I looked at Judy she stared at me with eggs around her mouth.

Black- (smiling) What?

Judy- You know what.

Black- No, I don't, and wipe that food from your mouth.

Judy- You're not taking my grandbaby anywhere.

Lily- Why, Nanny?

Judy- Well, because I'm taking you to go and see those really cool dinosaurs with the really big bones.

Lily- Yeah, I'm going with Nanny, Mommy.

Judy- Just bring us something back.

I began laughing because Judy never let me take my daughter anywhere. I had no idea why, but sometimes it made me wonder if she had any idea what I did for a living. I know I never told her. After breakfast Lily and Judy went to the museum as I waited for the group to come and get me. Eventually they did, then we were off to the clothing outlet. As we walked around in the outlet I couldn't help but to stare at Blue. She had long sleeves and jeans on when it was nearly 90 degrees outside.

Black- Red, what's with Blue and those hot clothes? She's melting.

Red- Blue.

Blue- What?

Red- What's with those clothes? You're smothering yourself.

Blue became upset and rolled her eyes, as she turned back around.

Red- Come on, let's check in this hippie store. They do be having some nice things.

Blue- Are you crazy?

Red- No, do you know how to dress? (She looked at Blue's clothes.) Oops, I guess not.

The clock had just turned to 11:00 P.M. as we pulled up in front of the club. Our sexy leather outfits resembled women with attitudes. Partying was least from our minds when it came to a job like this. We worked too hard and dangerous. Besides, it could be trouble most times. We walked over toward the door where a tall bouncer stood in the door.

Bouncer- Do you have identification on you, ladies?

Pink- What do we look young to you? That's crazy.

Grey- (poking the bouncer) May I see your identification, muscle boy?

Bouncer- Look, I don't want any problems, I just need to see it. Or else you'll be dancing in the streets.

Black- He's trying to play us. Just give him the IDs, Ashley. (She looked at Blue.)

Blue- Okay, if he wants it.

Blue stuck her hand in her chest, pulled out a gun, then pistol whipped the bouncer. He fell to the ground with his eyes rolling to the back of his head.

Black- Get him over there behind the dumpster. Hurry, before someone comes.

Pink, Blue, and Red did so then returned back to the door as I walked in. The party was very live as we searched for a table to sit down at. I noticed an empty table in the back so I headed for it with the rest following me. We sat down. A waitress walked over toward us with her pen and notepad.

Waitress- What can I get you, ladies?

Black- I'll take some buffalo wings and three shots of tequila. I'll take a lime and some salt on the side.

Waitress- Okay, do you want anything else?

Blue- I'll take a Scotch on rocks. The big glass, please.

Pink- I'll take three shots of Hennessey.

Red- I want three shots of tequila also.

Waitress- Alright, I'll be right back with your drinks.

Black- You know what I think? We should say our prayers now.

We all grabbed hands and put our heads down with our eyes shut. This was mandatory before every job. I felt like it would keep us in good hands.

Grey- Lord, we ask for your strength in the weak, your heart in our soul, your mind in our thoughts, and your forgiveness for our sins. Amen.

Black- Amen.

Pink- Amen.

Red- Amen.

Blue- Amen.

Just as soon as I opened my eyes Terrance stood at the door with a very pretty lady. What in the world was he doing here at a time like this? He never came to parties. My fetish for him overlapped that I had a job to do. Lights flashed on his smooth butter-like complexion as he smiled. He was interested in something that never crossed his mind. He then grabbed the woman he was with by the hand and headed to the middle of the dance floor. He began to look around once they reached then spotted me.

Grey- Black, you see what I see?

Black- Do you see what I see?

Grey- I sure enough do, that big tray of delicious free meats.

Black- No. (She elbowed Grey.) Look who's on the dance floor.

As everyone looked they noticed Terrance and the woman.

Blue- What the hell is he doing here, and who's he with? Did they come together?

Pink- Are you alright, girl?

Black- Of course I'm alright, what you mean?

Red- I can't believe him.

Black- (holding her hands up) Why are you guys tripping? He's not my man.

Grey- Well, you're the one who told us to look like he was.

Black- (sucking her teeth) Whatever.

Blue- Okay, everyone, just chill, here he comes.

Terrance and the woman walked over toward our table.

> Terrance- Surprised, huh?
> Black- (lifting her eyebrows) Sure, I guess.
> Red- What are you doing here? You don't know a thing about parties.
> Terrance- I know but it's worth a try. I'm surprised they don't have a guard at the door.
> Pink- So, who do you have with you?
> Blue- (shoving Pink's arm) How rude. (She looked at the woman.) Hi, I'm Blue. What's your name?
> Terrance- Her name is Samantha Blue and I'm getting married to her.

Pink, Blue, and Grey gasped then looked at me. I didn't tell them. I was too embarrassed because they knew I loved him and he was the only man I wanted. I felt like getting even because I felt like Samantha was the better woman. I hated her and I didn't care to know her.

> Grey- (whispering in Black's ear) You have to get him out of here… you can leave his bitch.
> Terrance- What might we be whispering about?
> Black- Excuse me, everyone (She stood up.) I'm ready to dance.

Blue and Pink stood up and moved out my way then sat back down. I walked over to some man standing in the corner. He looked decent enough to dance with.

> Black- (grabbing the stranger's hand) You want to dance?
> Stranger- Sure, I guess.
> Black- Let's go. (She pulled the man.)

I tried to get Terrance's attention by dancing sexy and honestly it worked. He watched me as Samantha watched him. She then became frustrated and pulled him onto the dance floor, standing close to me.

Samantha- It's getting a little hot in here.
Terrance- Here, let me take your jacket.
Samantha- Why, thank you. (She took off her jacket, looked at me, then swung her hair.)

Terrance walked over toward a chair then placed her jacket on it. I looked back at the girls to find them laughing.

Black- (whispering) Go do something to Terrance's car.
Red- What did she say?
Pink- I didn't hear her either.
Grey- I heard her. (She stood up.) Come on. Blue, you got your gun already so go talk to Mr. Mann.
Blue- Alright, I'll be waiting for you.

Blue went upstairs as Grey, Pink, and Red went outside. I continued dancing with the man. Meanwhile, Blue had just begun talking to Mr. Mann. He had sent his two bodyguards down into the party to have a couple of drinks. She sat with her legs open showing her panties and vagina area to him.

Grey- (standing in a phone booth) Hello, yes, I would like to report a Durango in the middle of the road of Park Avenue and Laims Road. It's on fire. (She paused.) I don't know whose it is, that's why I'm calling, now get here. (She hung up the phone.)

Grey, Pink, and Red ran to their jeep. Grey took the alarm off the car then opened the door. She grabbed four guns and masks, giving a gun and mask to Pink and Red. She then closed the door back and put the alarm on it. They headed back into the party. Grey walked over to the DJ.

Grey- Someone's car is in the road and it's on fire.
DJ- Okay, I'll announce it now. (He pulled the microphone toward his mouth.) Um, someone's car is on fire outside so go and check.

The crowd of people began to walk outside to see if it was their car on fire.

Samantha- You know what, Terrance, you should go and check just in case.

Terrance- I doubt if it's my car.

Terrance and Samantha walked outside to find his jeep on fire.

Terrance- What the fuck? (He ran to his jeep.)

After I noticed people running outside including the bodyguards I knew what time it was. Grey ran toward me and handed me my gun and mask. We put them on then ran for upstairs. We had to hurry before his bodyguards came back.

Samantha- (hand over her forehead) Who did this?

Terrance- (upset) Look at my car. Who did this?

We went door to door searching for Blue and Mr. Mann.

Black- Where is this girl?

Pink- Let's try the door in the back.

Grey counted to three then opened the door. Blue and Mr. Mann jumped as little children do when they're caught doing something wrong. He jumped up.

Mr. Mann- What the hell's going on here?

Pink- Shut up, fat ass.

Black- Where's the safe you always bragging about?

Mr. Mann- It's under the desk.

Black- If you're lying I will shoot your fat ass in the leg. (She looked under the desk to find nothing.) I warned you. (She let off a shot.)

The people that stayed in the party heard the shot and began running out the party. Mr. Mann's bodyguards heard the shot from outside so they ran inside the party.

> Mr. Mann- (holding his leg) Oh, shit. Damn. Okay, alright. Push the middle of the painting.

I could hear people screaming so I knew we had to hurry. I pushed the middle of the painting.

> Black- If the money's not here I'm going to shoot, your arm, foot, then ass.
> Mr. Mann- (in pain) No, it's all there, twelve thousand dollars.

As soon as the picture moved back Mr. Mann's money revealed. Grey handed me a bag to start stuffing the money into it.

> Pink- Hurry, I hear sirens.
> Black- Okay, I got it. Let's go. (She pistol whipped Mr. Mann.)

We began running down the halls trying to find a different way out without bumping into the guards. Just as soon as we turned the corner the guards began shooting at us. Grey fired back shooting both of them to their death. Before we ran down the stairs we took our masks off and put them and the guns in the bag with the money. We ran downstairs.

> Black- Alright, Pink, Grey, and Red, go out the back door. I'll go through the front and meet you in the back.
> Blue- Black. Make it.
> Black- I will now go. (She gave Blue the money.)

The girls took off. I walked out the front door as the sirens came closer and closer. We made it out just in time. I looked over and noticed that Terrance jeep was on fire. He was angrier than ever. He saw me then walked over to me. Samantha followed him.

Terrance- (angry) What's going on in there? Look what someone did to my jeep.

Black- (trying to hurry) Um, there's a shootout in there. Don't go in there, go home.

Terrance- Look at my car. How can I get home? I should have never come to this party shit.

Black- Look, make a report then go home. (She ran.) Take Sam with you.

Samantha- It's Samantha.

Black- (still running) Whatever. (She laughed.)

I ran to the back of the building and got in the car with the others and pulled off.

Black- Drive at a normal pace, everything is cool. They're just arriving.

We watched the police jump out their cars and run into the building as we drove past them. It took half an hour to get to the spot. The spot was our second home. It was where we went for privacy and a hideout after every job. The only people who knew about it were the group and Thomas. The drive to the spot was intense. Everyone was nervous but tried to maintain due to the others. Red's turns were too wide as she drove. Grey sung a song that none of us ever heard before. Pink rocked as Blue looked out the window. Soon the jeep came to a stop. I was so nervous that I didn't realize we were at the spot until Red mentioned it. We all got out of the jeep and hurried inside the house. Once Pink closed the door, Grey ran and jumped on the couch.

Grey- (jumping on the couch) We made it.

Pink- Thank you, God, for letting us make it. Blue, you freak. If your husband knew how freaky you were….

Blue- He does, that's why he married me. Speaking of him I have to get home. I told him I would be home at 1:30 and it's 12:56.

Red- Where's the control so I can lock the car up?

Grey- It's on the table.

Red- Do you guys have anything else to put in the car?

Black- Get the guns and masks.

Red walked out to the garage and put the guns and masks in the jeep then locked the doors. She then pushed the button on the control, which began turning the garage. As the jeep rolled in five cars rolled out. This was Thomas' invention he made for us. By the time Red came back in me and Blue were already dressed.

Black- Don't forget your pocketbook.

Blue- Oh, thanks. (She picked up her pocketbook from the chair.) I'll see you guys later. (She hurried off.)

Black- You don't want your money?

Blue- I'll get it later. (She opened and closed the door.)

Blue got in her car then headed home. About ten minutes later I left as the others stayed behind. The cool morning air must have encouraged me to sleep a little longer. I was so comfortable and relaxed that I didn't want to move. I was still tired from the job we had last night, because I didn't hear Judy come in the room.

Judy- (shaking Black) Black. Black. Have a late night last night? Do you want anything?

Black- (turning over) Sure. I could use a cold cup of water.

Judy- Lily was asking about you last night. You should spend the day with her.

She said she wanted a sleepover.

Black- (rubbing her eyes, smiling) I'll talk to her today. I think I will spend the day indoors, though. (She turned over to go back to sleep.) Right now I'm so tired.

Judy- Oh, yeah, someone wants to speak with you.

Black- (looking at the clock) 11:18 in the morning. Tell them I'll call them back later.

Judy- I think he wants to speak with you now. He said he'll wait until you wake up. Would you like him to wait?

Black- Who's he?

For a minute I was expecting Mr. Mann to walk through the door and kill me but instead Terrance walked in. My stomach jumped as I caught a flashback of last night.

Terrance- Are you dressed?

Black- Step out for a minute so I can slip something on.

Terrance- Alright, don't disappear. (He stared hard at Black.)

Judy- I'll grab you some water.

Terrance walked out of the room with Judy right behind him closing the door. I jumped up and threw on a pair of shorts, ran to the mirror and fixed my hair. When I felt that it was decent I opened the door back up and Terrance walked in.

Black- What's up? What are you doing here?

Terrance- I came to ask you about last night.

Black- What about last night?

Terrance- What the hell was going on? All I know is the DJ saying on the microphone calling my car out saying it's on fire. Then there are gunshots, people running, and screaming.

Black- I already told you what happened. Some guys were fighting which led to a shootout. Things just became a little out of hand.

Terrance- What were you doing inside then? Why did you come out so late?

Black- I didn't want to get shot. Would you? Why are you asking me so many questions anyway, what are you, a cop? (She noticed the phone ringing.)

Terrance- Well, do you know who did that fucked-up shit to my car? Whoever did it left me $10,000 on my doorstep today.

Black- No, I don't know who did that to your car. If they put money on your doorstep then why are you complaining? Most people wouldn't give you consideration. Why are you bugging me anyway? Where's Samantha, at home in bed? You have some nerve acting like you own me.

Terrance- I'm not acting like I own you. I was just worried.

Black- Well, don't be. (She stared hard at Terrance.)

Just then Judy walked into the room with my glass of water. She handed it to me, then stood there and smiled.

Black-Thank you. (She took a sip of the water.)

Judy- You're welcome. Is everything okay?

Terrance- Yeah, Ma, we're just talking. Could you please excuse me and Black?

Judy- (looking surprised) Well, pardon me. (She looked at Black.) Look, I know I told you to spend the day with Lily today, but we forgot about her going to Disney World with your Uncle Sam. They're leaving for three weeks.

Black- (putting her hand on her head) Oh, that's right. What time does she leave?

Judy- She leaves at four o'clock. It's eleven so you have time. Right now I'm going to get her three weeks of new clothes.

Black- Do you need money?

Judy- No, I got it.

Black- Is she still sleeping?

Judy- Yes, I'm going to wake her up, though. Talk to you later. (Before leaving she gave Terrance a kiss on the cheek.)

Black- (watching Judy close the door) Now what were you complaining about?

Terrance- I was not complaining. You know I thought I could come over and talk to you in a respectful manner and here you are knocking me. What's the problem? All I wanted to know was, were you okay? Is there something you want to talk about?

Black- I don't need to talk about anything, so on that note I'll see you later.

Terrance- What, you throwing me out?

Black- No, I'm kicking you out. Get the hell out.

Terrance- You know what? I thought that because we're good friends we could talk about anything. I remember when you were different but you've changed. What happened to sweet Black? The Black I used to go to the movies with? The one I used to play basketball with? Ever since I stopped coming over things have been different. My life has changed. It feels complete but empty.

Black- What does your feelings have to do with last night?

Terrance- (looking at the floor, hesitating) You know what? You're selfish and you don't have to worry about me worrying about you anymore.

Black- I thank you for your concern. Goodbye.

Terrance- (leaving out the door, then turning around) Maybe you need a good sticking to remove the bitch from your ass. (He turned around, walking away.)

I was surprised to hear Terrance talk to me that way. After all I was being a bitch but that was because of Samantha. I was completely jealous of her. She had what I wanted. I followed him down the stairs until he reached the front door than slammed it behind him. I peeked out the peephole to watch him leave but the phone began ringing. It was so aggravating that I had to answer it.

Black- (picking up the phone) Hello?

Red- Hello, Black.

Black- (mad) What!

Red- What's your problem?

Black- Nothing, I'm sorry. What's up?

Red- Look on channel 16.

Black- What's on channel 16?

Red- Just turn to it.

I grabbed the remote and turned on the television, turning it to channel 16. My heart fell to the floor as I noticed Mr. Mann.

Reporter- Yes, sir, could you tell us what happened?

Mr. Mann- Well, all I know is I was enjoying myself when four women busted in my office with guns and masks on. One of them shot me while they took my money. The woman that I had in my office was with them. She knew exactly what she was doing. Afterwards they hit me with the gun, and I have no idea what happened after that. They even killed my two bodyguards.

Reporter- Do you have any idea how they look?

Mr. Mann- No, I don't, only the one that was in my office. She better pray I never find her.

Reporter- That's all we have. Reporting from Channel 16 News.

I turned the television off and began laughing.

Black- I almost forgot about last night until Terrance came by.

Red- Did he ask about last night?

Black- He sure did. Wanted to know if I knew who set his car on fire. He's lucky I brought that $30,000 to him this morning.

Red- Was his car being on fire the only way to get him out the party?

Black- No, but I was also mad. We have to change Blue's hair color because Mr. Mann knows what she looks like.

Red- Yeah, I know.

Black- You guys still at the spot?

Red- Yes, we are. Blue came back about ten in the morning. She wanted to know if you were still here.

Black- Is she alright?

Red- Yeah, she's asleep. I told her I would call you. She looks like an angel. (She looked at Blue.) Bitch.

Black- (laughing) Leave her alone. I won't be over there until 6:00. Lily's leaving for Disney World with my uncle today. They'll be gone for three weeks.

Red- Lucky her. I know she's having all sorts of fun.

Black- Yes, I hope so. I'll be over later, though.

Red- Alright, I'll talk to you when you get here.

As I hung the phone up I noticed that Judy hadn't been taking good care of her plants that I gave her for Mother's Day. I went to the sink and inserted water into a drinking glass and watered both plants. Once that was done I placed them both in the windows where the sun beamed down. Once again I headed upstairs but couldn't succeed due to the doorbell ringing.

Black- (walking back down the stairs) Who is it? (She looked through the peephole in the door.)

As I opened the door a tall black man in his mid-twenties stood there in a blue Federal Express uniform. He had a computer board in his hand with a warm, friendly smile.

Black- (noticing his name on his shirt) Hello, Rodney, how may I help you?

Rodney- I'm looking for a Miss Black Cummings.

Black- I'm Miss Cummings.

Rodney- Might I add that you're a beautiful woman?

Black- Thank you very much. May I help you?

Rodney- I understand I don't make enough money for you, huh?

Black- Excuse me? What does money have to do with anything? Is

28

there something you have for me or are you wasting my time?

Rodney- I have one package for you. Could you sign where the X is?

Black- I don't remember sending off for anything. Do you know where it's from?

Rodney- No. Could you sign, please?

Black- Could you get the package?

Rodney- Right, I'll be right back. (He turned to get the package off the truck, then returned.)

Black- (finishing her signature, then taking the package) Have a nice day.

Rodney- You're welcome.

I closed the door in Rodney's face as he stood there smiling.

Black- (shaking her head) Stupid.

I had no idea where this package had come from. It was wrapped in the most beautiful wrapping paper ever. I wasted no time getting it open.

Black- (gasping) Oh my God.

I noticed a card that read: "To the most beautiful woman in the world. May her life be as beautiful as her smile." I smiled as if I were a little child with candy. They were the most beautiful earrings that I ever imagined. This had to be a mistake. I could tell real diamonds from fake ones and these were completely real. Once again I checked to see if there was a name but it wasn't. They sure were pretty, though.

Black- I'm keeping them.

CHAPTER 3

I went back upstairs and fell to sleep. I hadn't realized that it was 4:00 P.M. until Judy called me, so I jumped up grabbed the new hair bow that I bought for Lily at the mall and ran downstairs.

Black- (wiping her eyes) I'm coming.

As I reached the living room Judy and Lily sat on the couch waiting. Lily was all packed and ready to go.

Judy- The dead has arisen.
Black- Stop it.
Lily- (running to Black) I'm leaving, Mommy.
Black- (picking Lily up) I know, I'm going to miss you so much. (She squeezed Lily tight.) Are you going to miss me?
Lily- I sure enough am.
Black- (putting the new hair bow in Lily's hair) Here, I bought you this so that you won't feel alone. This is so I'll always be with you.
Lily- (smiling, hugging Black) Thank you, Mommy, it's so pretty.
Black- You're welcome, baby. What time is Uncle Sam coming?
Judy- He said....

Suddenly the doorbell rang.

> Judy-Here, he is right on time.
> Lily- (opening the door) Hi, Uncle Sam. I'm so glad you're here. Let's go.
> Uncle Sam- Well. (He laughed.) Go get in the back of the car.
> Lily- (running to the car) Yeah.
> Judy- So how are you, Sam?
> Black- Yeah, how are you?
> Uncle Sam- Fine. (He kissed Judy on the cheek, then Black.) This trip is going to be perfect for Lily. We'll try not to take too long. No longer than three weeks.
> Judy- Hey, you may be my brother but Black and I will jump you over that little girl.
> Uncle Sam- Oh, I don't want that.
> Lily- Come on, Uncle Sam. Please. (She was using her puppy face.)
> Uncle Sam- (throwing his hands up) Oh, alright, alright. Let's go. (He walked over, picking up Lily's bag.)
> Black- Here, let me help you. (She picked up Lily's other bag.) Uncle Sam, I want the both of you to have a safe trip.
> Uncle Sam- You know she's in the best hands right now.

We walked to the car and put Lily's bags in the trunk, then Uncle Sam closed the trunk back. He then gave me another kiss then got into his car and started it up.

> Lily- Goodbye, everybody, see you later.
> Uncle Sam- (pulling off) I'll call you.
> Judy- (waving) Okay.

I watched until I couldn't see them anymore. I know Lily was in the best hands but this was the first time I let her out of my sight for three weeks. I was going to miss her so much. What would I do for these next three weeks?

Judy- She'll be alright. She'll love it.

Black- (grabbing Judy by her arm) Oh, yeah, let me show you something.

I pulled Judy into the house then ran upstairs in my room and took the earrings from the dresser.

Black- (walking down the stairs) Did you order anything from a catalog?

Judy- No, I don't recall.

Black- Are you sure?

Judy- Yes, I'm sure.

Black- (pulling the earrings out) Well, look at these.

Judy- (gasping for air) Oh my God, they're beautiful. They had to cost a fortune. Where'd you get them?

Black- Some man from Federal Express brought them here today. He must have had the wrong address. The only thing was it had my name on it.

Judy- Are you giving them back?

Black- Should I?

Judy- (hesitating) I won't tell if you don't.

Black- That's a deal.

We locked our fingers together to reassure a promised secret.

Judy- (closing the door) They sure are pretty. You sure someone who admires you didn't give you those earrings?

Black- Have you ever seen me bring a man in this house?

Judy- No.

Black- Well, then I don't have a secret admirer.

Judy- Alright, but people just don't mistakenly receive ten-thousand-dollar earrings. (She laughed.)

Black- (laughing) You got jokes, huh? Let me go upstairs and get dressed. I got to go.

Judy- (letting her laugh die down) Where you going?

Black- Me and the girls are going to catch a movie and relax.

Judy- Well, then we can go out tomorrow and get something to eat. We can also go to the movies.

Black- Okay. (She kissed Judy on the forehead, then headed upstairs.)

Meanwhile, back at the spot....

Pink- What makes you think that I don't have heart?

Red- I know you don't. You're a pussycat.

Pink- Oh, please. Try me to do something. Anything, I'll show you.

Red- Oh, yeah? (She was thinking.) I know what.

Pink- What?

Red- Nah, I don't think you can handle that.

Pink- What? I know I could.

Red- You positive?

Pink- Shoot.

Red- I dare you to....

Pink- To what?

Red- I dare you to ask Black how it felt to be raped.

Pink- Are you crazy? She never talks about that and now you want me to bring it up. Are you crazy? She'd kill me.

Red- Just like I said, you're a pussycat. You're scared of her.

Pink- No, I'm not.

Red- Then prove it.

Pink- Well, are you scared of her?

Red- Fuck no.

Pink- Well, neither am I.

Red- So then prove it.

Just then Grey walked into the kitchen at the end of the conversation. Pink and Red just stood there smiling.

Grey- What?
Pink- Nothing.
Red- Nothing.
Grey- What time did Black say she was going to get here?
Red- About 6:00 P.M.
Grey- Well, I'm going to get us some goodies and something to cook.
Tell Black I'll be back.

Grey grabbed her car keys and left out the door. Red looked at Pink containing to get her point across. Pink smiled and shook her head. She was down with it.

Pink- Shall we tell the others?
Red- (shaking her head no) No.
Pink- (smiling) You little bitch.

I had just finished getting dressed as I walked down the stairs and into my jeep. I loved how the Lord blessed me with money, family, cars, and life. Even though I wasn't living the best life right now I couldn't complain. Even if I wanted to get out Thomas would kill me first. The drive from my house to the spot was about a half an hour. I pulled off. I loved how the city flowed. It was so energetic and live. The sight of celebrities and fine men was to kill for. As I came to a stop sign two women in their mid-thirties began fighting on the hood of my car. People began to gather around the fight from the sidewalk.

Black- What the hell? Get off my car! Fight on the sidewalk.

I felt a speck of sweat form on my nose. That normally was a sign for when I was mad. My temper switched faster than a light. I pushed on the gas and took off with the women still on the hood of my jeep. They held on tight. I turned the corner and spotted a group of bushes. That only encouraged me to drive faster, so I did. As soon as I was two feet away from the bushes I stepped on the brakes and watched the two ladies fly into them.

Black- (putting down her window) I said get off my car.

I drove away fast. The two women continued to fight in the bushes. It was so funny that I had to laugh. As I pulled up to the spot I noticed Grey's car missing. I parked and went into the back trunk and took out a suitcase then closed it back, and went inside. Blue was the first person I saw as she slept on the couch. I walked over toward her and put the suitcase on the floor next to her, then sat down next to her. Something had to be wrong because she still had on the same clothes from last night. I looked around to see if I saw the others but they weren't.

Black- (shaking Blue) Blue. Blue, you alright?

Blue- (waking up) Huh? (She yawned.) Oh, you're here. What's up?

Black- You alright?

Blue- Yeah. Just a little tired.

Black- Well, something must be wrong if you're still in those same clothes from last night. You want to talk? You know I'm always here for you, right?

Blue- I know. I know.

Black- Well?

Blue- (sitting up) Where are the others?

Black- I don't know.

Blue- Come on, let's go in the bathroom.

We got up from the couch, walked upstairs and into the bathroom.

Black- (closing the bathroom door) What's the problem, Blue?

Blue- Felix and I are having marital problems. I think he's cheating on me.

Black- Are you cheating on him?

Blue- No.

Black- No. Blue, you know better than that.

Blue- Black, lower your voice and you know that's not my style. Now if you can't listen then I'll go to someone who will. (She was getting emotional.)

Black- Okay, I'm sorry. After all, what do I know about men?

Blue- Look, don't knock yourself like that. All I'm saying is that I need you to listen. Can you do that?

Black- Yeah. Go ahead.

Blue- Well, like I was saying. Felix has changed. We hardly do anything but just stay in the house. Early this morning I got this phone call from some unknown bitch talking about "tame your dog, Blue." How the fuck she know my name? I confronted Felix about it but he just denied it. We had an argument so I left.

Black- Damn. You sure you don't know who the girl is?

Blue- I mean it felt as if I heard the voice before but I'm just not sure.

Black- (taking a deep breath) So what do you want to do find out who she is?

Blue- No. We don't need to make the problem worse. I just wish that I could find someone who would be cool and real. I know that sounds like a fairytale but you never know. Could you imagine taking a roughneck mother fucker and turning him into still hard but a loving and understanding man? Wouldn't that be nice?

Black- Wouldn't it? Sometimes I wonder if you and Isles would have made it.

Blue just stared at me as I went into the past. Blue and Isles met while working for Thomas. They tried not letting their personal life mix with business but eventually they weakened. They fell in love and remained in love for several years. One night we went on a job that required everyone. Somehow the job got all screwed up and we had to get out fast. Thomas and my group got out in time but that left Isles and his group inside alone. He didn't have any backup, and Thomas wouldn't let us back inside the building. I never heard Blue scream so loud as we pulled her in the car before the police arrived. She didn't want to leave him but Thomas couldn't care less and threatened our lives if we didn't. He just took the group of men that Isles was training and put them into work as another group. She hated Thomas from that day on. The men who owned the place that we robbed killed Isles' men but couldn't handle him. Isles killed two men and couldn't make it out in time before the police arrived. They sentenced him to six years in jail with life parole. It was such a tragedy to see wonderful people torn apart. They had plans of getting married and having kids. That was six years ago. She tried to hold on to being faithful as long as she could but she couldn't manage, so she left him. One year later she met Felix and they hit off so good the following year they got married. Blue- Do you know from all these years I still love him? I think about him every day. Like if he didn't go to jail how many kids would I have. Or would I still be working for Thomas? I know we would have been married already. Shit, that man probably hates me for what I've done to him. I straight abandoned him. I would pick Isles over Felix anyway but I already committed to my vows.

> Black- Isles don't hate you, he understands what you had to go through. There's no way in hell you would have been able to manage this job and stress about Isles.
> Blue- Maybe you're right. He'll always be my baby. Something tells me that when he comes home Pink will be back on her devious mission.

Pink had a huge crush on Isles even though she knew he and Blue were together. She didn't care. Once the two of them were very close to fighting over him until we broke it up. The two of them just haven't been the same since then. They only put up with each other because of the job.

> Black- (laughing) You better not say that too loud or she might hear you.
> Blue- (laughing) I know.

Suddenly a loud bang approached the door, which sent our hearts to the floor and back.

> Pink- You guys alright in there?

I looked at Blue confused and hard. It felt as if Pink heard everything that we said. I opened the door. Pink and Red stood there with weak smiles.

Red- What's wrong?

Pink- You two okay in there?

Blue- Yeah, we were talking but now we're finished.

Red- When did you get here? I didn't know you were here until I saw your jeep outside.

Pink- We were getting dressed.

Black- Where's Grey?

Pink- She went down town to get some goodies.

Black- That's my girl.

Red- Are you two finished, because I just made a strawberry dipped cake. I know you all want some.

Black- Yeah, we have to change Blue's hair anyway because Mr. Mann remembers her. I have the suitcase downstairs. By the time Grey gets back we'll be done.

CHAPTER 4

Meanwhile, Grey had quite a selection of junk food in her cart. It would cure the side-effect of smoking marijuana.

> Grey- (looking in her cart) Now let's see. We need something a little different tonight. Spaghetti. No. Steak…no. Maybe chicken. Nah.

Then Grey spotted a big tank full of lobsters. They were huge and completely different. It was a great idea. She pushed the cart over toward the tank where a female worker greeted her.

> Worker- Hi, how are you today?
> Grey- (smiling) Fine and you?
> Worker- Pretty good, I can't complain. What can I help you with?
> Grey- Yes, can you tell me how much five lobsters would cost?
> Worker- (looking on a price sheet) About thirty dollars apiece. So that's one hundred and fifty dollars. Is that okay?
> Grey- Yes, I'll take it.

The worker walked toward the tank and took out a lobster. It was so huge and plenty of meat per person. She was so fascinated that she wanted to see it up close.

Grey- May I see it up close, please?

Worker- Sure.

The worker held the lobster over the counter as Grey studied it. Somehow Grey forgot about the real world and went into a daze. About five seconds later she was frightened from the back. She was too frightened to turn around. When she did she was surprised from the sight of Isles.

Grey- (screaming) Oh my God, Isles. What the hell? (She put her hands over her mouth.) God.

Isles- Give me a hug, girl.

Grey gave Isles a hug so tight that his insides nearly popped out.

Grey- When did you get out?

Isles- Earlier today. My ears were itching so that means someone was talking about me.

Grey- Maybe someone was, but it sure is good to see you.

Isles- I was trying to get in contact with Thomas. Do you know his cell phone number?

Grey- Yeah. It's 718-0009. Can you remember that?

Isles- 718-0009. That's easy.

Grey- I'm so happy to see you, Isles. Do you need a ride or something?

Isles- No. I'm here with my cousin Lisha. We're going to chill to-night. Then I'll see what's up with Thomas. Don't tell him I'm home.

Grey- No problem.

Isles- So how's the group?

Grey- Any one in particular?

Isles- I know Blue's okay. Her husband better make sure of that.

Grey- Oh, so you heard? I thought you didn't know. News does travel in jail, huh? Would you like to join us in dinner? I could get another lobster.

Isles- No, I'm fine. I'm going to eat with my cousin, but I'll see you later. Tell everyone I said hello and don't tell Thomas I'm home.

Grey- Okay. (She gave Isles a hug.) I'll see you later. Be safe.

She couldn't wait to get back to tell the others the good news. As she opened the front door and headed in the living room she found the girls feasting on strawberry dipped cake. She almost didn't recognize Blue because of the different hair color and style.

Grey- Blue, great hair, and would you guys stop ruining your appetites? The food's here. Guess what? I have some good news. You have to guess.

Red- Come on, that's not fair, just tell us.

Grey- Nope. You have to guess. Come on, stop being lazy.

Pink- Okay, you found a boyfriend.

Grey- No.

Black- You're getting married.

Grey- No.

Blue- You're pregnant.

Grey- Yeah, right.

Red- You're a man.

Grey- Bitch, please. You guys are so pathetic. I mind as well just tell you.

Red- Well, spit it out.

Grey- Guess who I ran into today?

Pink- Who?

Grey- Isles.

Black- (excited) For real? I must have talked him up.

I looked at Blue to see that she acted as if she didn't hear what Grey said. She seemed rather nervous. She smiled once she recognized Pink looking at her from the corner of her eyes.

Grey- He said hi to everyone, even you, Blue.

Blue- Oh, yeah?

Pink- I'm pretty sure he doesn't know she's married.

Grey- Yes, he does and (looking at Blue) he said your husband better take good care of you.

Black- Is he coming over here? He better be coming to see us.

Grey- No, he's coming tomorrow. Don't tell Thomas he's home, okay? He doesn't want him to know yet.

Red- You think he's going to work for Thomas again?

Black- I don't know. Men do what they want, when they want. They're hard headed.

Blue- Isn't that right.

Pink- (jealous) Don't we have some cooking to do? (She headed off to the kitchen.)

Grey- (shrugging her shoulders) True.

We all headed into the kitchen. I glanced from the corner of my eye and caught Blue laughing.

Blue-Oh, I have a surprise but I need some help carrying it in. (She went back out the door to the car to get the groceries.) Pink, help me.

After a while Pink and Grey came in the house with the groceries.

Red- What did you get?

Suddenly we heard some rattling in the bags.

Blue- What the hell is that?

Grey- What does it look like? It's lobsters.

Pink- I heard they scream when you put them in hot water.

Grey- We'll soon find out.

The theory on lobsters screaming when being put into hot water was true. We ate, straightened up, then began our night. The living room was where we had our meetings and also our relaxing resort.

Black- Did Thomas call today?

Red- Yeah, he's going to meet us at the Loxus dinner tomorrow. We have to be there by 10:30 A.M. He said he has another assignment for us.

Black- Everything there?

Red- Ten in the flesh.

Black- Blue, you finish rolling up yet?

Blue- Sure enough. I'm sparking up first. (She put the lighter to the marijuana.)

Grey- (picking up the liquor from the table) Let's try not to get too fucked up tonight.

Pink- You just hurry up with that liquor.

It was wonderful how close to sisters we were. We've been good friends for seven years. I've been through thick and thin with these women. When Thomas first introduced me to them I knew I wasn't going to like them but boy, was I wrong. Nothing could come between us. About three hours later we were so drunk that all we could do was joke and laugh. I hadn't noticed how Red kicked Pink's foot. That was a sign for her to exploit the dare.

Pink- (clearing her throat) Girls, I think that we need to become a little closer.

Grey- Like?

Pink- Like, that we know each other but we could become a little closer.

Grey- (intoxicated) I hope not sexual, because I swear I like men. (She laughed.)

Pink- No. I bet that every one of us has a little something inside of us that's concealed. Never talked about. Do you dare? Do you dare to speak about the truth? Whatever we talk about is between us and when I say between us I mean it or else. You know what I'm talking about.

Grey- So, you're talking about sharing information so forbidden, that if any one of us told anyone, we would kill them?

Pink- Yeah, my point exactly. We're too close to even think like one of us would tell each other's business. So what do you say, girls?

The room went quite for a moment. She was asking us to do some real deep shit I could say. I knew every one of us had secrets at the bottom of the closet.

Grey- If everyone knows the consequences, then I'm in.

Blue- I don't know if I want to tell you anything because....

Pink- You're scared, huh? Why, when everyone's going to know something about everyone? Even Black. (She looked at Black.) Right? Put your girl on. If we can't trust each other now, then when?

Black- Well, if it's like that then we're going to start with you, Pink.

Pink- Fine. Make sure your girl's down for the cheese.

Blue- I'm in. Let's hear it, Pink.

Pink- Where should I start?

Blue- How about I ask you a question? Cool?

Pink- How about then I'll ask you a question? Cool?

Blue- My question for you is, what happened to you and James?

Pink went into shock. How dare Blue ask her that question? Three years ago Pink and James met. One year later they became serious and planned for a wedding once Pink got pregnant. They were happy. A situation went down to where they separated and Pink got an abortion at five months pregnant.

Pink- (looking upset) If you tell I'll kill you.

Blue gave Pink a smile that could kill the whole world.

Pink-Well, as you all know James and I were in love. Everything seemed so perfect like a fairytale in a book. It was no problem because we had that type of relationship. (She hesitated.) One night he got a phone call in the middle of the night. I was upset when he said his mother wanted him. I trusted him so it was no problem. When I noticed he was gone for two hours I decided to take a trip to his mother's house. When I talked to her she told me that she hadn't seen or heard from James since the last time we all had dinner together. I was madder than ever. On my way back home I spotted his car at a hotel. I knew it was his car because of the license plate number. I found which room he was in and threw a brick through the window. When I pulled back the curtain in the room I saw it.

Blue- You risked your marriage for a stupid bitch, and she didn't have it like you. James had crazy dough.

Black- She might have her reasons but I would have given him another chance.

Pink- You guys are missing the point. You don't leave your man for another chick but what if it's the other sex?

I pretended to choke while Grey turned her head. That's why Pink never mentioned it. She was too embarrassed.

I couldn't even picture myself with a woman. I'll pay someone else back, though.

Blue- You mean to tell me the cake mix is not all that?

Black- (laughing) Stop it, girl.

Grey blurted out with a laugh so hard and attractive we followed. I know Pink was mad but the fact of another man taking your man was funny.

Pink- (mad) Oh, yeah, what about you, miss(putting her head to the ceiling) angel?

Blue- (looking intoxicated) What about me? What could you possibly ask?

Pink- Let's talk about your mother hating you and you loving two men.

Red- Now we're getting personal. (She laughed.)

Pink- Well, let's hear it, Blue.

Blue- Everyone knows that I love my husband, Felix. I'm completely over Isles....

Pink- Cut the shit, Blue. You know you love the hell out of both men. Especially Isles. You used Felix as a cover-up for Isles. Admit it and stop playing games.

Blue- (forming tears) So what! I love two men. Especially Isles. You claim I'm an angel, huh? Did you know that I used to sell my body to eat? My mom was so fucked up on crack that she didn't care what the hell I did or ate. I had to provide for myself basically hooking. That's how Thomas found me. You think it took me a while to jump on this opportunity. Even you know this opportunity was fucked up. I have a son, and he's seven years old. His name is Derrick. Usually when most kids fuck up and they're parents is doing drugs the parents straighten up. Not my mother. She let them put my little boy in a foster home, and she moved away. I don't know where he is. I just know he's in Durham. Did you write it down, Pink?

Time went by as Grey revealed that she wanted to have a family in a year with the older man she's been seeing, and Red revealed wanting to be with women. It was my turn. I prayed no one asked me about my sex life.

Pink- Black, it's your turn and my question to you is (hesitating), How did it feel to get raped, and would you have sex again and who would you consider for the job?

Black- Wow, that sounds like three questions in one. Well, I don't ever want to experience that again. I wouldn't even wish that on my worst enemy. Could you imagine some stranger you don't know or have any control over raping you? Not knowing how it feels or if he has a disease. (She shook her head.) If only I could find him I would kill him right where he stood. I don't think I can feel for sex but if I did....

Blue- Spit it out, girl.

Black- I would consider Terrance for the job. He thinks I need it anyway.

We met early that morning at the Loxus diner. I felt uncomfortable about sharing forbidden information. The others were, too. Red and Pink seemed to themselves and sat with Thomas on the other side of the table. I caught Pink staring at Blue but when she noticed I was looking she smiled at me then turned her head. I wondered how long the men group was going to be away because I was rather used to them.

> Thomas- How's everyone doing this morning?
> Red- Better than ever.
> Thomas- (admiring Red) Good. Blue, I love the hair. As you know it's time to go back in. I've found something pretty interesting. Can I count on my girls to do the job? I know I can. Now here's what we're going to do....

My mind couldn't concentrate due to last night. I don't know why I felt like this but I just did. I turned my head and looked at the entrance door. No sooner later Rodney walked through the door. He was alone and I'll tell you without that Federal Express uniform on he was handsome. I watched a female waitress escort him to his table. I couldn't help but to look. He sat down and became comfortable. He began looking around as he smiled and I prayed he didn't see me. I had no luck whatsoever because he did. He waved as if he knew me. I just put my head down and pretended to hear Thomas.

> Blue- (grabbing Black's arm, then whispering to her) When I advise you to take precaution, please promise me that you'll play it cool.
> Black- (whispering) Yeah. What's up?
> Blue- (whispering) I'm serious, Black.
> Black- (whispering) Yes. Now tell me.
> Blue- (whispering) Look behind you slowly.

When I turned around Terrance and Samantha shared a gorgeous breakfast table. I turned around quickly and became frustrated. I hated that woman with a passion.

Black- (whispering) Why the fuck they always have to be where we at?

Suddenly the perfect idea struck me. I could try to get him jealous. I turned to see if Rodney still was looking at me. He was so I smiled at him and waved back. I could hear Blue laugh a little. She knew exactly what I was up to.

Blue- Sneaky bitch.

Maybe Rodney wouldn't eat breakfast alone after all. Thomas stopped talking.

Thomas- Any questions?

I had no idea what the hell was going on but I just shook my head no anyway.

Thomas- We'll meet tomorrow and go over it again. Now if you'll excuse me I have some important business to discuss.

Red and Pink moved out the way so Thomas could get out. He walked over to another table where a couple of businessmen sat and joined them. Red, Grey, and Pink sat at another table leaving Blue and me alone.

Blue- Is it me or those bitches acting funny?
Black- Grey spoke. I'm not the one to kiss anyone's ass anyway.
Blue- I don't know what the problem is but....

I don't know what it was about that diner but everyone seemed to be there. Isles had just walked in the door. Blue hadn't noticed because she was too busy running her mouth. I couldn't wait to see the expression on her face once she saw him.

Black- (putting her pointer finger to Blue's lips) Don't talk. When I tell you to play it cool do so. Okay?

Blue- My husband?

Black- Girl, just turn around.

Blue turned around and almost lost her breath. She saw Isles but he didn't see her. She turned around quickly and began to panic.

Black- Calm down, girl. It's going to be alright.

Blue- What should I do? Sit here, right?

Black- Yes.

Blue got up and ran into the bathroom. I couldn't help but to smirk because it was a little funny. Isles looked around until he saw Thomas. He then walked over to the table and tapped Thomas on the shoulder. I turned back around to look at Rodney finding him in a conversation with Red. He must have felt me staring at him because he turned his head and looked at me. I didn't want her to think I was interfering. Rodney then stood up and walked toward my table and sat down. I could see the how embarrassed she was so I pretended not to see her. Meanwhile….

Isles- Excuse me, Thomas, could I talk to you for just a moment?

Thomas- Excuse me, gentlemen. I'll be right back. (He stood up.)

Isles and Thomas walked over toward the corner where no one sat.

Isles- I was waiting for you.

Thomas- That's exactly what you'll do. Wait. Don't you ever in your life come looking for me. I run the show, not you.

Isles- (shaking his head) Hold on. Hold on. Hold on. You're the one who told me that you would come and get me this morning before you came to breakfast so we could discuss this. I was supposed to have my three million last night. I just did six years for you, Thomas, and lost everything I had. Including people. I don't want to work for you anymore. I just want my money so I can go.

Thomas- (smiling) Alright, I'll tell you what. Come and do dinner to-morrow night with me at the Highly Brothers diner. About seven o'clock and I'll have something worked out for you.

Isles- (taking a deep breath) Okay, tomorrow at seven o clock. (He walked away.)

As Isles headed for the door to leave Pink went up to him and greeted him. Isles was rather upset hoping it was Blue instead.

Pink- Isles. How very nice to see you. You're still looking better than ever. May I have a hug, please? (She was making a puppy face.)

Blue peeked out the bathroom just in time to catch the hug. Her heart sunk into her chest as she felt depressed. Isles released the hug then left. Red was still mad. She could not believe that Rodney just did that to her. I didn't realize that she saw Blue peeking out the bathroom, so she got up went over to the bathroom door and pushed it in, hitting Blue in her face. Blue fell down to the floor on her back. Everyone in the diner heard the door hit her in her head so they all ran to the bathroom door.

Red- Oh my God, Blue, I didn't know you were back there. I'm sorry. Are you okay?

Blue- (on the floor) Oh, my head. You tried to kill me, Red.

Red- No, I didn't. (She helped Blue up.)

I also heard the loud bang so I ran over to the bathroom to make sure everything was okay. I had to squeeze through the crowd in order to get to Blue. She stood in the mirror with her hand on her forehead. Pink just sat down unconcerned. Thomas was madder than ever. He felt that we were acting like little kids around company. He eyed Grey hard. That was a sign for her to get us in order. She got up from the table and pushed us inside the bathroom, then closed the door.

Grey- Look, I don't know what the problem is but you guys better cool it. Thomas is mad and you all know what happened last time he was mad.

Red- Well, bitches don't know how to let shit be. You knew I was talking to him first, Black. You don't know a thing about dick.

Black- Neither do you. You prefer pussy pies.

Grey- Cut it out. God, we're supposed to be sisters and you're acting like enemies. I've never heard you talk to each other like that before. What's the problem? Ever since last night I've felt this problem with you guys. We should have never even shared that kind of information.

Red- Black just told my business. We're supposed to kill her.

Grey- Then I guess we're going to kill you, too.

Blue- (looking in the mirror) All I know is that my head hurts. I look like someone kicked me in my face. Is it bad?

Black- Is it?

Grey- So are you guys going to cool it or what?

Black- I'm going home before I smack that bitch.

Red- Whatever.

Blue- Me and Grey rode here with Red and Pink. Can I get a ride to the spot to get my car?

Black- Come on. (She walked off.)

I was so mad I could bend steel. How did this occur? It was wrong of Rodney to just get up and leave her without telling her excuse me but that wasn't my fault. Maybe I should have not looked at him. I wasn't interested in Rodney, I just wanted to use him to get Terrance jealous, who happened to be looking at me as I walked out the diner. After I dropped Blue off at the spot I went home. As I pulled up in front of my door Judy was on her way out.

Judy- I thought you weren't coming back today.

Black- Where you going?

Judy- To the movies and dinner, you coming?

Black- Yeah. Did Lily call? I miss her already? We might as well take my car, it's easier.

Judy- (getting in Black's jeep) No, not yet. It's still early. Maybe by the time we're back.

I pulled off. I couldn't wait to tell Judy what had happened today. I would wait until after the movie. After the movie we went to a beautiful restaurant. I still was upset about earlier so I didn't eat much.

> Black- (tampering with her food) Judy, you're not going to believe what happened today.
> Judy- You and the girls had a fight.
> Black- (looking shocked) How'd you know that?
> Judy- I've known you for a very long time. I can tell when you're happy, mad, or sad. You're like the daughter I've never had.
> Black- (smiling) That's why I love you. I just don't know how this all happened. Red's mad because some guy she wanted to talk to wanted to talk to me, Pink's fighting with Blue over Isles, Blue's husband is cheating on her.
> Judy- What about Grey?
> Black- She's the only one with no problems.
> Judy- Well, you know sometimes your friends could be the worst enemies. Especially females. I know when a woman wants something so bad she will do just about anything to get it. Always keep your guard up. Always.
> Black- (taking a deep breath) That's right.

Meanwhile, after the meeting at the diner, Thomas called Pink, Grey, and Red into his office. The door closed. A conversation took place that only the four of them knew about. About a half an hour later Grey stepped out the office leaving the others inside. She looked back at them then closed the door. She was petrified. God only knew why. She ran out the building and down the street. She began crying. She ran faster passing people, cars, and policemen. Her legs somehow developed to run even faster so she did. She fell but picked herself up and continued to run. Finally she spotted an alleyway so she ran up it. Once she got halfway up it she stopped running and began walking fast. She listened carefully to see if she heard a sound. She did, so she stopped and listened. Scaring the daylights out of her a black cat ran from behind a dumpster. It scared her so she walked even faster. She didn't realize she stumbled over someone's foot until she noticed she was on the ground. When she looked back it was bum sleeping on the ground.

Grey- Oh, I'm sorry.

She was a little relieved but still worried. Where was she going to go? How was she going to get there? She took a couple of footsteps ahead to think. She had no idea the bum was standing up behind her so she continued to think. Then he pulled out a gun with a silencer on it. She had no idea what was coming her way. As the bum took his last step behind her he stepped on some glass. The sound of the glass breaking made Grey turn around. Out of nowhere the bum shot her twice in the face. Her vision abandoned from her eyes as she died lifelessly on the ground. She was dead. The movie and dinner was fulfilling. We had a marvelous time. We were both tired and full so the bed seemed to be our best friend. As I was putting the key in the door I heard the phone ring so I hurried to answer it. I just knew it was Lily. I got the door open and ran to the phone.

Black- (picking it up) Hello?

The news I received was horrible. Who would ever expect a phone call saying that one of your best friends was dead? I couldn't believe it. My mouth opened as tears hatched in my eyes. I fell to my knees and dropped the phone. I heard Judy close the door then run to me. She got on her knees then hugged me.

Judy- (scared) What wrong, Black? Tell me, baby. What happened?

I cried even harder.

Black- Grey's dead. She was murdered in an alleyway. (She was crying harder.) Oh my God.

Judy- (hugging Black tighter) It's okay, baby. It's okay. (Her tears were forming.)

I was taking Grey's death hard for the past week. Today was the day of her funeral and I wasn't really in the mood but I had to pay my respects. It was the first time I saw the others since she died. I listened as a family member of Grey's sang Amazing Grace. She sounded just like an angel. I felt as if it was a message from the big man upstairs. Telling us to get our life together before it's too late. One thing about Grey was that she didn't have a lot of family. The group was her family. Maybe that's why she wanted to move away and start a family of her own. I looked over and caught Red and Pink sharing jokes. Once they noticed I was looking at them they pretended to feel sorrow. I felt as if something was wrong. Though I had on the shades to prevent people from seeing my tears it was no use. I didn't care who saw me cry. I loved that girl. Terrance and Samantha stood behind me. I couldn't take them standing behind me at a time like this. I knew Blue and I would have it out for her not coming to her best friend's funeral. That was just unacceptable. My emotions were running wild and I didn't know if I could handle it. I felt as if I were being watched. Uncomfortable you could say. I waited impatiently for the service to end. Thomas and Isles stood in the back. I wondered if Thomas gave him his money yet. I hope Isles wasn't coming back to work for Thomas. He should just stay out while he has the chance. The service ended. I hurried along because I didn't want to stay for food or conversation. Judy must have felt the same way because she was right behind me. She didn't even talk to Terrance and Samantha she just waved and smiled, but kept walking. I reached my jeep and went to take off the alarm. I was tapped on my shoulder from behind. I turned around to find that it was Rodney dressed up in a suit.

Black- (sucking her teeth) What do you want? I'm not in the mood.
Rodney- Well, I didn't get a chance to talk to you before you just ran out on me.
Black- (rolling her eyes) Your point?

Judy- Look, sorry to interrupt your conversation but it's chilly out. I want to get in the car.

I took the alarm off so Judy could get in the car. She did then close the door.

Rodney- Look, I understand that you're going through a hard time right now but I was just wondering....
Black- If you can hit it? If we can lay up in a hotel and get high? What exactly is it? Why are you here anyway? You didn't know her.
Rodney- I saw it on the news and I just want to make sure that you're okay. She seemed like a nice friend.
Black- You sound stupid and you look like a stalker. Leave me alone.

I walked away from him and got into my jeep. I never noticed how I dropped my wallet on the ground as I pulled off. Just when Rodney thought things couldn't get any better he looked to the ground and saw it. He walked over to it and picked it up. He opened it and smiled. It gave him the perfect opportunity to come to my house. He walked away and looked up to find Terrance looking at him. Rodney smiled but Terrance didn't smile back. Samantha was watching Terrance from the corner of her eyes.

Samantha- Is everything okay, Terrance?
Terrance- Yeah. Everything's fine. Let's go.

I didn't go to the gathering at Red's house because I wasn't really in the mood. They called me several times but I told Judy to tell them I was sleeping. I missed Lily already. She's been gone for a week and a half. I decided I wouldn't tell her about Grey's death until she came back. Here it was nearly twelve in the morning and I couldn't sleep. Just as soon as I began to doze off the doorbell rang. I got up out my bed and headed for the stairs. Judy poked her head out her bedroom door.

Black- I got it.
Judy-   Who is it?

Black- I don't know but they better have a good excuse for stopping by twelve in the morning.

I opened the door and became very disappointed. The last person I wanted to see was Rodney.

Black- Have you lost your mind coming here this time of night? What do you want?
Rodney- I have something for you.
Black- What, another package?

He dug in his inside jacket pocket and pulled my wallet from his coat.

Rodney- You dropped it after the funeral.
Black- (taking the wallet) Thank you, I appreciate it. Do you know what I would have lost in this? Thank you once again.
Rodney- No problem. Look, I know that you're probably not in the mood, but I was wondering if you and I could do dinner. No, I don't want to hit or lay up in a hotel getting high. Though it does sound like a good idea.
Black- What?
Rodney- I'm just playing.
Black- I don't know....
Rodney- Please don't say no.

I couldn't help but to just stare in those deep brown eyes. He was so attractive, polite, and ongoing. I could tell that he was not going to give up unless I went to dinner with him.

Black- Alright. Tomorrow at eight. Is that good?
Rodney- Yes.
Black- No friends, gold teeth, gangster chains, or anything else.
Rodney- (laughing) No problem. Tomorrow at eight, don't be late.

Black- Goodnight.
Rodney- Goodnight.

I closed the door. Was I sure of what I just did? I wanted to give him a chance any way, plus I've never been on a real date. I walked back upstairs. I thought Judy closed her door but she didn't. She stood there smiling.

> Judy- Give that man a chance. Every man deserves a chance. When he messes up (balling up her fist), mess him up.
> Black- (smiling) Goodnight. Talk to you in the morning.
> Judy- Alright. (She closed her door.)

I'd waken up early that morning. Since Lily was away I had no responsibilities. That felt weird but free. Nothing seemed better than a hot shower so I took one and went to make breakfast. As I got in the kitchen Judy already sat at the table with breakfast already made. She even put me a plate on the table so I could eat.

> Black- Smells good. (She kissed Judy on the forehead.) What are you doing up so early?
> Judy- I have a doctor's appointment. Sit down and eat.

Just as soon as I went to sit down at the table the doorbell rang.

> Black- I'm going to take this bell and throw it. Who is it?
> Stranger- I'm looking for Black Cummings.

When I opened the door a black man in his thirties dressed in a suit stood in the doorway.

> Black- May I help you?
> Stranger- Hi, my name is Detective Cargo. I'm with the NYPD. (He showed Black a badge.) I'm looking for Black Cummings.
> Black- What are you looking for her for?

Detective Cargo- Are you her?

Black- Yes, I am.

Detective Cargo- Yes, I'm investigating a homicide. I believe that you and Grey Prescott were good friends? Correct?

Black- The best.

Detective Cargo- Sorry to hear about your friend. I won't bother you long. I just have a couple of questions.

Black- About?

Detective Cargo- Your friend. Do you know any of her old boyfriends?

Black- No. Why?

Detective Cargo- I don't know how to bring this to you but I'm pretty sure you know your friend was murdered. We don't know who it is yet but one thing I could tell you is that it isn't an ordinary person.

Black- What do you mean?

Detective Cargo- Well, I mean whoever it was knew her.

Black- (shocked) Are you sure?

Detective Cargo- You tell me. If you were carrying 30,000 dollars on you and someone robbed you possibly killed you why wouldn't they take the money?

Black- They would.

Detective Cargo- My point exactly. They didn't, though.

That was really strange. Why would she be carrying so much money on her anyway? Everything was charged to her card she never carried cash.

Detective Cargo- Do you have any idea why she would be carrying so much money on her anyway? I mean, I would never carry that much money on me, especially the city. (He looked at his pad.) I believe there are three other women that she was close to.

Black- Excuse me?

Detective Cargo- Do you know a LaRed Barkman at 48 Parasite Road, Pink Weathers at 136 Butterview Park, and Blue Chancer at

493 Mavis Hill?

Black- Yeah. We're pretty close.

Detective Cargo- Do you know a good time I can reach them?

Black- Well, you have their address. If you'll please excuse me I have some breakfast to attend to. (She closed the door, then took a deep breath.)

Judy- Who do you know that would want to kill her?

Black- I don't know but something's not right.

Thomas had given us a call for a meeting later on that day. I hated to say it but the group wasn't the same. The absence of Grey was recognizable. I missed her so much. Her chair sat empty and quite. The way everyone was acting was as if I were the only one who cared. We had been at this meeting for almost an hour and Blue still didn't look at me or say anything. Thomas had another assignment for us. I felt unsure. For one we were a person short and our friendship changed since that night. I was paying no attention whatsoever to Thomas. I didn't care to hear what he had to say. Pretty soon he stopped talking and Blue hopped up. She thought I was going to let her get away just like that but I followed right behind her. When I noticed we were out of Red and Pink's sight I tapped her shoulder. I could tell she didn't want to turn around but she did.

Black- Some friend you are. How you not going to come to your best friend's funeral? You were supposed to pay respects to her but it's too late. You'll never see her again.

Blue- Well, I didn't want to see her in a casket. That's for sure.

Black- Well, I guess if something happens to me you won't be coming to mines either, huh? Why are you acting like this and why are you dressed like that?

Blue- So you got jokes, huh? Keep it to yourself. (She walked away.)

I couldn't believe what was happening. Everything was falling apart. How could this happen in a week? Did I have bad luck or something? Pink and Red walked up behind me as I watched Blue pull off.

Red- Is everything okay?

Black- Yeah. What you guys up to?

Pink- Oh, nothing. We called you several times but Judy said you were sleeping.

Black- I was. How was the gathering?

Red- Fine. What you doing tonight? Let's go to a movie.

Black- I'm going to have to take a raincheck on that. I have so much to do.

Pink- Okay, maybe another time.

I walked away and got into my jeep then pulled off. The day went by so fast that I almost forgot that I had a date. A dolphin water fountain poured as we ate. Rodney was a complete gentleman. He made me want to understand men. He had given me the impression that he wanted a close friend. I felt so sorry for how I acted toward him these past couple of days. His smooth butter-like complexion asked to be to be touched, and boy, did I want to touch him.

Rodney- So Black, are you seeing someone else?

Black- Not at the moment. I'm not really looking.

Rodney- Someone as beautiful as you wouldn't want to be on a pedestal?

Black- I am on one from myself.

Rodney- Independent. I like that. (He looked at Black.) God, you're so beautiful. I have to stop looking at you. You're too sexy. I love those earrings also.

Black- Thank you.

Meanwhile, Red, Pink, and Kilin sat on a stoop outside on a dark street. They had all been drinking and they seemed to be pretty drunk. Kilin was Red's associate in the streets. She also had a bad reputation because she was laid by every man in town. She hardly had any friends. Mostly all the girls around hated her.

Pink- Kilin, is there anyone around here that you didn't sleep with? Your ass is stretched all over this world.

Red- (laughing) That's not nice, Pink. Leave her alone. If she wants to be a hoe let her be a hoe.

Pink and Red laughed so hard that they almost fell off the stoop to the ground. Kilin didn't laugh because she didn't think it was funny.

Kilin- Ha. Ha. Ha. Very funny. Why I never see you with a man, Pink?

Pink- Well, 'cause you're giving away free ass and men do want it. (She was laughing.)

Red- (laughing) Oh my God.

Once again Red and Pink began laughing. Kilin didn't realize that Chelsey was coming down the street because her back was turned. He was considered a no-minded person. What I meant by that was that he hardly was paid any attention to. He had a couple of marbles loose so everyone stayed away from him. Kilin realized Pink and Red eyes were looking at something so she turned around. She realized it was Chelsey.

Kilin- Oh, look at this ugly mother fucker. Beasts do walk at night-time. (She was laughing.)

Pink and Red became quiet and stopped laughing. They felt as if something was going to happen. Kilin didn't have to bother that man because he wasn't bothering her. He walked on. They thought he paid her no mind until he came back and pistol whipped Kilin then ran. Pink and Red followed right behind him but ran to her car. The two of them jumped in the car and sped off, leaving Kilin on the step looking as if she passed out from being drunk.

Pink- Oh my God, did you see that?

Red- Yeah. I loved it. He knocked her out. Kilin runs that mouth too much.

Pink- Take the back roads. We're going back to the spot.

Red made a right turn and drove into town. Pinks spotted me in the restaurant. At first Pink thought she was seeing things but she had to be for sure.

Pink- Hold on. Stop the car. Back up.

Red- What did you see?

Pink- Look, just back the car up.

Red did so. I had no idea that the two of them sat there and watched me eat dinner with Rodney. Red became so furious that she forgot she was driving.

Red- That bitch.

Pink- She didn't give it any time. Did she?

Red- We can fight fire with fire. Trust me.

After we ate Rodney insisted that we go to a dance club. I really did not want to go but I also didn't want to sound like a party pooper. We sat at a table and watched people dance and communicate.

Black- I'll be back. (She stood up.)

Rodney- Okay. I'm going to get some drinks.

I squeezed my way through the crowd as Rodney went and got our drinks. When I entered the bathroom two women stood in the mirror powdering their faces. One was tall and light skinned and the other was short and dark skinned. I just walked over to another sink and began looking in the mirror. I began playing in my hair to make sure that I looked just fine. I turned and looked at the women that were already in the bathroom. I found them looking hard at me as if I just did something wrong to them.

Tall female- You think you cute, huh?

Short female- I don't know why 'cause (imitating the movie) you sure is ugly.

They began to laugh so hard that I became annoyed. I couldn't let my true colors show so I just laughed along with them.

Tall female- She's laughing. She must know it's true.

Black- (looking at the tall female) You know. You look hungry. Your man must not have any money. (She picked at the female's figure.)

The short female laughed as if she'd watched a funny movie. It seemed rather funny to her.

Black- I just know you're not laughing because I know your man has a lock on the refrigerator. Say it with me. Slim Fast.

I guess I pushed her buttons because she ran over and spit in my face. I thought that was the nastiest thing you could do to a person. I took the short female's shirt and wiped my face with it.

Black- You done fucked up now.

I balled my fist up and punched the short female in her face so hard that she fell to the floor. The tall female grabbed my hair and began pulling it hard. I screamed and kicked her in her stomach. She held her stomach and fell onto the sink. Once again the short female jumped on me and pulled me to the ground. She then began kicking me several times in my back. That also gave the tall female time to get to me. They both kicked and stomped on my back. The pain went from my back to my head. I tried to get up but I couldn't. I began to panic. I kicked my leg into the short female, which caused her to fall face ward into one of the toilet stalls. I grabbed the tall female by her shirt to help me gain my balance and pushed her on top of the short female in the stall, causing the short female's head to be pushed inside the toilet. She kicked as if she was drowning. I just held the both of them down and began pounding on the tall female until she was knocked out. I threw her to the ground. The short female took her head from out the toilet and took a deep breath. I kicked her in her face so she wouldn't get back up and she didn't. I was completely out of breath. Those two gave me the fight of my life and it was all over nothing. I inhaled deeply until I caught my breath then fixed my hair. Before I left out the bathroom I closed the bathroom stall. As I walked out the bathroom Rodney sat at a table waiting with our drinks.

Rodney- Is everything alright?

Black- Yes, I'm fine.

Rodney- For a minute I thought you fell in.

Black- No, not me. What did you get me to drink?

Rodney- Cranberry and vodka good?

Black- Yeah, thanks.

Rodney- You like the club? I usually come here when I'm uptight and need a drink.

Black- I like it. It's very nice. I should come here more often. Do you have any children? Sorry if I'm being nosy but that's just me.

Rodney- I don't mind. I wish I had a family, someone to occupy my time, and talk about. Maybe if I find that woman.

Black- (clearing her throat) That's nice.

Rodney- Do you have any children?

Black- (smiling) Yes, I do, a six-year-old daughter. Her name is Lily.

Rodney- Really, how beautiful.

I kind of liked Rodney for what kind of man he was. It also seemed to me that he was very patient. Most men weren't programmed with patience. I looked at him as he watched other people dance. He just smiled and moved to the music. Then his eyes told me that he had just seen something.

Black- What's wrong?

Rodney- I think your friends from the funeral is here.

I turned around and found that Samantha and Terrance were sitting and chatting at a table across the room. They didn't recognize me and that's the way I wanted it to remain.

Black- Well, they're not really my friends. We just know each other.

Rodney- Oh. (He was trying to understand.)

Just then a scream came from out the women's bathroom. Rodney and I turned to the bathroom. A woman in her mid-twenties ran out the bathroom looking frightened.

Woman- Someone call an ambulance. Get help!

Just then people began running in the bathroom. That was the perfect excuse to get away.

Rodney- I wonder what happened.

Black- Me too. Look, Rodney, it's getting late and I have to go home.

Rodney- Well, I'll take you home.

Black- No, that's okay. I'll be just fine, thanks. (She left.)

I caught a cab home. All I could think about was how I ran out on Rodney. That was the second time. I doubted if he wanted to see me again. The following morning I woke up to my phone ringing.

Black- (picking up the phone) Hello?

Red- Good morning, sleepy head. Did you forget we have a job to do this morning?

Black- What job? I didn't know we had a job to do this morning. Besides, it's 7:40 in the morning.

Red- I know. We're supposed to be there by 8:00 A.M. Hurry up and get dressed, we'll be outside waiting. We're going to take Pink's car.

Black- Where's the job?

Red- At the Leer building.

Black- Okay. (She hung up the phone.)

I regretted not paying attention at the meeting. I had no idea what was going on. As I got in the car, I could see Blue looking at me from the corner of her eyes. Maybe she wanted to apologize. Then again maybe not. When we arrived at the Leer building Thomas waited for us in his limo. He flagged us to come inside his limo, so we did.

Thomas- I thought I told you all to be twenty minutes early.

Red- We had to pick up Black. She overslept.

Thomas- (giving Black the evil eye) Late night?

Black- Something like that.

Thomas- Alright, girls. Here's what's going down. There are thirty-seven floors in this apartment complex. The owner also lives in this building and he's filthy rich. He stores his diamonds on the third floor in a safe. The room number is 3b. I was unable to get the combination to the safe, so Red, you're going to have to blow the safe. (He handed Red a time bomb.) Richie is going to meet me on the fifteenth floor, so that means every floor I'm on you're on the second floor up until you reach the third floor. Once you have the diamonds you have to leave from that floor going down the fire escape you came up. (He handed each girl a tracker.) Here, these will switch the tracking once you throw them in the elevator. Don't get in the elevator, just throw the trackers in then go down the fire escape. Be careful and watch each other's backs. I'll see you in a little while. (He got out of the limo.) Pink, back your car into the fire escape so it will be easier to get away. (He walked away.)

Pink got out the limo right behind Thomas and closed the door. Thomas walked inside the building as Pink went and backed her car by the fire escape.

She accidentally backed into the fire escape too hard and rubbed the paint off onto it.

Pink- Damn.

We were watching from the limo.

Blue- What the hell is she doing?

As soon as Thomas entered the building we got out his limo and headed for the side where Pink and the fire escape was.

Pink- How will we know when he's on the fifteenth floor?
Red- We can see him. (She pointed.)

Soon Thomas was on the fifteenth floor.

Black- It's show time.

We entered the building and began destroying cameras, computers, and alarms. People that got in our way we shoved in bathrooms and kept it moving. Finally we were on the third floor.

Blue- There it is, room 3b. Get it, Red.

Blue never realized she dropped her tracker on the next floor up.

Blue- Shit. I dropped my tracker.
Red- You better go get it before Thomas leaves.

Blue headed back upstairs for her tracker. Red kicked in the door with the diamonds, ran in and placed the time bomb on the safe. She then activated it and ran back outside the door.

Red- Get out the way!

The sound of the loud explosion caused several people to scream. Red ran back in and picked the diamonds up out the blown safe, then ran back out and pressed the elevator button. We waited for the elevator door to open. I had no idea that a security guard was sneaking up behind me with his gun pointed. Pink was watching the whole thing. She put her gun down and pretended not to see the guard. Hardly did she recognize Blue behind her until the bullets flew past her and into the guard. He dropped with little movement. I jumped and turned around finding the guard behind me on the floor. He was going to kill me. Pink looked back at Blue and gave her a weird smile.

Red- It's open. (She threw her tracker in the elevator, then headed down the fire escape.)

The rest of us threw our trackers in the elevator then followed Red down the fire escape and into the car. Meanwhile, in the camera room showed four people in the elevator.

TV man- They're moving down in the elevator now. They're going to the first floor.

Several guards with guns surrounded the elevator on the first floor. They were waiting for the elevator door to open. Impatiently they waited. When the doors opened the guards looked confused. There wasn't a soul in the elevator.

Guard 1- (on his radio) We've lost them, sir.
TV man- (on his headphones) That's not possible.
Guard 1- There's nothing here but trackers.
TV man- Shit! (Upset, he threw his headphones.)

We made it out just in time. Forty million in diamonds. Life didn't get any better than that. I still couldn't get over the fact that I had almost gotten shot. That never happened to me before. Blue must have still been a little shaken up about it because she hadn't said a word since we left. She didn't even look at me. I wondered what was going through her mind. As usual Red and Pink decide to stay behind at the spot. Blue was really avoiding me because she just jumped in her car and headed off. I jumped in mines and followed right behind her. At first she had no idea that I was behind her until she looked in her rear-view mirror. Once she spotted me she began to drive faster so I sped up to her. She then tried to lose me by making short turns, but I just kept right up on her tale. I then became side by side with her by driving to oncoming traffic and ran her car off the road. I stopped my car and got out. Blue opened her car door and got out looking madder than ever.

Blue- (walking to Black, yelling) What the hell is your problem? Are you crazy? You tried to kill me.

Black- What's going on with you?

Blue- I'm going to kick your ass, bitch.

Black- If you think you're bad enough come do it.

Blue- (walking up to Black) Oh, yeah. (She smacked Black.)

When she hit me I almost forgot that she was a good friend of mine. I practically went insane. Her anger had reached appoint of insanity itself. We fell to the ground with pounding fist as cars past by as we fought, not even daring to stop. Finally it was over due to us being tired. I still had the best of her, though.

Black- (tired and out of breath) Now are you going to tell me what's wrong or do I have to kick your ass some more?

Blue- (tired) You make me sick sometimes. Are you blind, do I have to point it out? Black, something's not right. I can feel it.

Black- What's not right?

Blue- Everything. For one where is the men group? They've been missing for a very long time. I'm still getting those aggravating calls. Grey. I loved the hell out of that girl. I feel so stupid I didn't make it to the funeral but best believe that I loved her. I hate myself for not making it to the funeral but I just couldn't stand seeing one of my girls in that casket. I thought that day wouldn't come until we were at least sixty. How can one person just be here today and gone tomorrow?

Black- Shit, the fucked-up thing is that we have to all be inside a shitty-ass casket. All of us, Blue, even you. You think that most of those people we kill family can stand being at funerals? No. No one can but you have to be there to give respect and love.

Blue- Black, Pink just was standing there when that guard was creeping on you. She just stood there and watched. I went back to get my tracker from the next floor up. The only thing was it was on the stairs. If it would not have been on the second floor you would have died, because I would have not been there in time to save you.

Black- Are you sure? I mean, why would Pink just stand there and let me get shot? It doesn't sound right. Thomas even said the men are just fine and they will be back shortly. I just don't know what to say because I'm shook up about it just as well. Listen to yourself. Do you really know what you're saying?

Blue- Fine, you don't have to believe me. (She stood up.)

Black- (standing up) I didn't say I don't believe you, it's just that….

Blue- What?

Black- (taking a deep inhale) You know what we need? A little vacation. I have an idea.

I decided to take Blue on a double date to Dorney Park with Rodney and me. She really didn't want to go but eventually I changed her mind. My dad took us to this park all the time before he died.

Blue- I really don't think I should be going on this little vacation. How many days are we going to be gone for?

Black- Three days. Put your bags in the back.

Blue- I'm really not in the mood to be anywhere with Felix. Especially public while we're fighting.

Black- Who said I was bringing Felix? There you go, always assuming things.

Blue- You're not bringing him?

Black- No.

Blue- Well. Who did you call on the phone?

Just then Rodney drove up to my house with Isles behind him.

Blue- (surprised) You're bringing Isles?

Black- Why, you don't want to go?

Blue- Hell yeah. (She sat in the front seat of Black's jeep.)

Black- Hey, just put your cars in the garage with Blue's and lock the door.

Rodney and Isles parked their cars in the garage then got out. They went to the back of their trunks and grabbed their luggage then headed toward my car. Rodney almost forgot to close the garage door so he ran back and did so. Once the door was down he locked it.

Isles- (walking over to Black) Is everything alright?

Black-   More than you know. We're all ready so put your bag in the back.

As Isles put his bag in the back of my jeep I got in the car. I leaned over to Blue to find that she was completely nervous.

Black- Calm down and get in the back with Isles.

Blue- What? No, what are you doing?

At that point Rodney was nearly twenty feet away from the car, carrying his luggage.

Black- Rodney, put your bags in the back and sit in the front with me. Let Blue sit in the back with Isles.

Blue got out the front seat and sat in the back as Isles opened the door on the other side. They both got inside and closed the door. Blue looked out the window to keep from looking at him. Rodney put his bags in the trunk then closed the door. He walked to the front seat of my jeep then got in.

> Black- Rodney, this is Isles and Blue. Isles and Blue, this is Rodney.
> Blue- Hello. How you doing?
> Isles- What's up, man?
> Rodney- How's everyone doing?

On our first day away we spent time looking at museums and plays, the second day was a day of shopping and working out in gyms followed by warm hot tubs, and the third day we reached Dorney Park. I've never seen a child smile bigger than Blue. She loved every moment of it. Especially that her and Isles was catching up on old times.

> Blue- Wow, this place is huge.
> Rodney- I hope you guys know how to have some fun. Where should we start?
> Isles- You know what? To make it simple let's start with the smallest ride here.

The first ride we went on was the bumper cars. That was my favorite ride when I came here with my dad. We were having so much fun that the day was just slipping away. The time came to where we had to go and only had time to get on one more ride.

> Blue- Well, we only have time for one more ride. Which shall it be?
> Rodney- I pick the biggest roller-coaster.
> Isles- I second that.
> Black- Oh. No.
> Blue- I'm too scared to get on that roller-coaster.
> Rodney- Now look. The only way to say we came to this park is to get on that big roller-coaster.

Blue and I hesitated but got on the ride to look good for the men. As we waited for the people that had just gotten on to unload Terrance and Samantha walked off the ride. I wanted to turn my head but something wouldn't let me. I wanted him to see Rodney and me together. I wanted to make him jealous. Terrance began walking and turned to find me standing there next to Rodney. He smiled and walked over toward us.

> Blue- (waving) Hi, bitch.
> Samantha- What? You don't even know me.
> Blue- I don't have to know you.
> Terrance- Cool it, Blue. How you doing, Black?

I just walked away from him as if he said nothing and ignored him until the ride began. I know he was embarrassed. I was so happy he saw me with Rodney. After the ride we all purchased pictures of our faces as we went down the rollercoaster .We headed back to Manhattan. As we pulled up to my house Judy was outside pacing back and forth. She seemed to be paranoid about something. I prayed it wasn't Lily. I parked the car then got out.

> Black- What's wrong, Ma? What happened?
> Judy- Where have you been? You didn't tell me you were leaving for three days.
> Black- I know, it was kind of unexpected.
> Blue- Is everything alright?
> Judy- Whose cars are in the garage?
> Blue- Mine.
> Rodney- Isles and mine also. Why, did something happen?

Judy put her head down so I knew that meant yes. We all ran for the garage door. I pushed the button and waited impatiently for the door to open. When it did our mouths dropped. Rodney, Isles, and Blue cars were ruined. The windows were broken out and the paint was scratched off. Every last tired on their car was flat.

Isles- What the fuck is this?

Blue- (surprised) Oh my God. (She goes into tears.)

Isles- Look at this shit. Who did this?

The sight of their cars was such a tragedy. Isles- How did this happen?

Black- (looking at Judy) Did you lock it?

Judy- Yes. This didn't happen until last night because the cars were fine yesterday and the day before.

Blue began crying even harder. I felt bad for everyone. I really didn't know what to say.

Blue- My husband is going to kill me.

Felix- Hi, hun.

Blue turned around quick to find Felix standing behind her. He was so mad that his eyes were nearly bloodshot red.

Judy- I was going to tell you he's been here for the past three days looking for you.

Felix- Took a little vacation? (lighting a cigarette) I didn't know anything about this. Why wasn't I informed?

Blue- Well, baby, you see....

Felix- I don't want to hear it, just get in the car. My car. (He was being sarcastic.)

Blue got her things from the back of my car then got in Felix's car. I felt horrible as he rolled his eyes at me. I turned my head and looked to the ground. I was too embarrassed to look at Rodney or Isles. What the hell was going on? It was going on four days and situations were getting complicated. Rodney or Blue didn't call me in four days. I knew they were mad at me. I missed Lily so much. I wished she could just reach out and give me a hug right now but I knew that was impossible. Thomas mustn't have had any more jobs because he hadn't called either. Judy and I was sitting in the living room reading magazines when the doorbell rang. I was praying that it be Rodney or Blue but instead it was that aggravating detective.

Detective Cargo- Hi, how you doing?

Black- (aggravated) Fine, I guess. What do you want?

Detective Cargo- I'll make this brief. I went to your other friends' houses and only one of them answered. Do you know a better time I could reach them?

Black- What do I look like, their keeper?

Detective Cargo- Look, I understand that you don't feel like being bothered, but did you know your friend was pregnant when she died?

I froze. Did he say pregnant? Who? When did this happen and why didn't she tell me? Why would she keep this from us?

Detective Cargo- I detect you didn't know.

Black- Why didn't you tell me before?

Detective Cargo- I didn't know until the autopsy.

Black- Well, I didn't know. (She was in disbelief.) She kept a secret from us.

After the detective left I decided to pay Red a visit. When I arrived she seemed rather nervous when she answered the door.

Red- Black. What are you doing here?

Black- I just came to check on you. I haven't seen you in a while. What's up?

Red- Nothing. Just relaxing.

Black- Everything okay?

Red- (looking back into her house) Um. Yeah.

Black- Oh. Okay, I'll make this brief. Some detective came to my house....

Red- (interrupting) Cargo.

Black- Huh?

Red- Detective Cargo, right?

Black- Oh, he talked to you. Did he tell you Grey was pregnant?

Red- (shocked) Yeah, right.

Black- Yeah.

Red- Why didn't she tell anyone?

Black- I don't know but that's not like her. What did he talk to you about?

Red- Look, not to be rude but I'll call you later and tell you everything. Alright?

Black- Okay. Make sure you do.

I walked away and got in my car as she closed the door. She headed back into her bedroom and closed her door. She had a woman sitting on her bed with a matching bra-and-panty set waiting for her.

Red- You comfortable, Londa?

Londa- Yeah, I'm comfortable. Who was at the door?

Red- No one important. Where were we?

Londa- Come get in the bed.

I went and paid Pink a visit but no one answered, so that left me with Blue. I was so scared to knock on her door because I just knew she was mad at me. After all it was my idea. I knocked on her door and waited for someone to answer. A couple of seconds later Felix opened the door.

Black- Is Blue here?

Felix- Yes, but she's sleeping. It's best if you let her sleep. She's wild when you wake her.

Black- Well, when she wakes up just tell her I came by and to call me.

(She walked away.)

Felix- I'll be sure to. (He closed the door.)

I kind of felt a little relieved that Felix didn't have an attitude with me. Maybe him and Blue patched things up after all. As I pulled up to my house I noticed Terrance's Durango parked outside. He had changed it to a different color and put twenty-four-inch rims on the wheels. I knew he had full coverage with his insurance company but the money I gave him would perhaps make him forget about the incident. I wished to God that Samantha wasn't inside but as to my luck she was. As I walked in the house she sat in the living room laughing with Terrance and Judy.

> Judy- Oh, Black, you're here. I was looking for you. Do you know where the cornmeal is?
>
> Black- I used it all after I cooked fish last night.
>
> Judy- Well, could you run out and get me some more? Thanks, you're a lifesaver. Terrance, I have to speak with you in private. Samantha, would you like to ride with Black? That would be nice.

How could Judy do that? I hated Samantha with a passion and Judy was asking her to ride with me. I was hoping she would say no but instead it was yes. I hated every moment of it. I decided to go to the shopping store to get the cornmeal and a couple of other things. It wouldn't be long before we were there.

> Samantha- So what is it that you do for a living?
>
> Black- Why do you want to know?
>
> Samantha- Well, because I see you have a mansion, a nice car, and I know that you're loaded or you wouldn't be in a mansion.
>
> Black- I don't believe that's any of your business.
>
> Samantha- Well, I'm an elementary teacher, and I don't make half of what you make or I would be in a mansion.
>
> Black- Well, you could say I'm a taker. I take whatever I want when I'm told or when I want I want it. Alright?

Samantha- What exactly does that mean?

Black- Nothing. I guess it's over your head.

Samantha- You don't like me very much. Do you?

Black- No, but my opinion is weak.

Samantha- Your opinion is strong. I know you and Terrance are best friends and you have been for a long time. He always talks about you.

Black- He does?

Samantha- More than you know. He loves you like a sister. I know how much he means to you and I would be fool to try and take that away. I mean you'll always be friends. I love that man more than anything on this earth and I will keep him happy till the end. I just hate when people prejudge me because I'm a good person inside.

Black- I believe that you are, but if you hurt him mentally or physically (looking at Samantha) I'll kill you.

I couldn't help but to feel guilty about not liking Samantha. I doubted if I wanted to call it truce, though. She had something I wanted. Dinner was ready as we sat around the table hungry. I still hadn't said a word to Terrance since he'd gotten here. I'm pretty sure he knew I was mad.

Samantha- (eating) Judy, this food is marvelous. You have to cook for me. Will you cook for the wedding?

Judy- (smiling) That's a great idea. I'd love to.

I thought to myself oh great, there goes that stupid wedding. I doubted if I would attend. I knew Lily would make me. One way or the other. Just as I put my first fork full of food to my mouth the doorbell rang.

Black- I'll get it.

I walked over to the door then opened it.

Rodney- Are you busy? If so I can come back another time.

Black- Oh. No. I thought you were mad at me.

Rodney- For what, you didn't do it. Whoever did, though, better pray I don't find them.

Black- I was just about to eat dinner. Would you like to join me? If not I understand.

Rodney- Don't be silly.

Black- Come in.

Rodney walked inside then I closed the door behind him. This was great because I didn't feel so bare. I had a date also. I didn't realize how evil Terrance eyed Rodney.

Black- Rodney, this is my mom Judy, her son Terrance and his soon-to-be wife Samantha.

Rodney- Hi, how you doing?

Black- Everyone, this is Rodney. He'll be joining us for dinner. (She sat down.)

Judy- (standing up going into the kitchen) Let me go and get you a plate so you can eat.

Rodney- Thank you. (He sat down.) You cooked, Black?

Black- No. Judy did.

Rodney- Everything smells so wonderful.

Terrance- Shouldn't you wash your hands before you eat?

I couldn't believe Terrance said that. Rodney just stared at him then smiled.

Rodney- You're right. You can't trust people these days. (He looked at Black.) Where's your bathroom?

Black- It's upstairs on your right.

Samantha was mad as hell. Terrance could see her looking at him from the corner of his eyes but he didn't care. Judy came back from the kitchen with Rodney's plate.

Judy- (looking at Black) Did your friend leave?
Black- No. He's washing his hands.

Soon Rodney returned from upstairs and joined us in dinner. I knew misery
was in the air and I loved it. An hour went by and we were fuller than ever.
Rodney hadn't said a word since he came back from the bathroom. Maybe he
was enjoying the food or Terrance made him mad.

Judy- (finishing up dessert) So Rodney, did you enjoy the food?
Rodney- As a matter of fact I did and I would love to do this again.
Judy- Well, you're welcome back in my home any time you like.
Rodney- In that case I will most certainly take a raincheck. (He stood
up.) I have to go but I really loved your cooking, Judy. (He walked
over, giving Judy a kiss on her cheek.) Thank you.

I stood up and walked Rodney to the door. Terrance leaned over and mumbled
to Samantha.

Terrance- That's just like a nigger. Eat and run.
Samantha- What's your problem?
Terrance- Nothing. Why?

Rodney opened the door walked out then turned around.

Rodney- You know, I don't think your friend likes me too much.
Black- I guess his wife is starting to get to him. You're welcome over
anytime you like.
Rodney- That's good to hear but to make things a little more com-
fortable, how about dinner at my place?
Black- Your place?
Rodney- Yes. I promise I won't bite unless you want me to.
Black- Don't worry. I got my nine at my side if I need it.

Rodney thought that was so funny being that he didn't know what I did for a living. He didn't know I was serious.

> Rodney- (letting his laugh die down) You're too funny, girl. So to-
> morrow night at eight o'clock, is that good?
> Black- I'll see you then. Bye. (She closed the door.)

I really was starting to like Rodney if I was going to his house. Normally a person would have to shoot me to go inside a guy's house, but Rodney was different. Very different. I was so full and tired that I couldn't do dessert. I began walking up the stairs.

> Judy- Going to bed, Black?
> Black- Yeah. I'm tired. Just call me when you're finished and I'll come
> and clear the table.
> Judy- No. You go ahead to bed. Samantha and I will clear the table.
> Black- Okay. See you in the morning. (She walked upstairs.)
> Terrance- Ma. I'll help you with the table.
> Judy- No. Samantha will do. Come on, honey.

Terrance got up and started walking up the stairs.

> Samantha- Where you going?
> Terrance- To the bathroom, then we're going home.

Meanwhile, I was getting undressed in my room and ready for bed when Terrance walked past my door. I had no idea he was watching me. Every move I made aroused him in every way. He began breathing heavily as he watched. Somehow he lost his balance, causing him to stumble into the door. He hurried and ran into the bathroom then closed the door. My heart jumped as I walked to the door and looked out. No one was there so I closed and locked it then went to bed. The following morning I woke up to a phone call. It was just the person I wanted to talk to.

Black- (tired, picking up the phone) Hello?

Lily- Mommy, Mommy, you sleeping?

Black- (waking up) No, not at all. You okay, baby?

Lily- Yeah, I'm fine, Ma. I'm having fun, I love it. I got on all the rides.

Black- You did? That's good. Where's Uncle Sam?

Lily- Trying to kick it to some lady.

Black- Where'd you learn that?

Lily began laughing.

Lily- Uncle Sam taught me that.

Black- (laughing) Well, put him on the phone.

Lily- Uncle Sam, my mom wants to talk to you.

He continued to harass the woman. She was pretty tired of him herself. She wasn't even close to being interested. Lily put the phone down from her ear and walked over to him then punched him in the stomach.

Uncle Sam- (losing air from his lungs) What you do that for?

Lily- My mom wants to talk to you.

The woman that he was harassing gave Lily a high-five, as he took the phone from Lily's hand.

Lady- That's exactly what I was thinking.

Lily laughed as the woman walked away.

Uncle Sam- Hello? Hello?

Black- Uncle Sam, what are you teaching my child?

Uncle Sam- If anything she's trying to get me hurt. We're having a good time, though. Can you believe she thinks we got on all the rides?

Black- Well, just keep her happy.

Uncle Sam- No problem, you know all the women think Lily is just the most adorable thing. Not me personally.

Lily- I heard that.

Uncle Sam- I'm just kidding. Just playing.

Black- So when will you be back?

Uncle Sam- In two weeks.

Black- Are you sure?

Uncle Sam- Maybe.

Black- Well, just hurry up. I want my baby home.

Uncle Sam- I will. Where's my sister? She's not out tricking, is she?

Black- (smiling) Oh, I'm telling you said that when she wakes up.

Uncle Sam- You better not. Tell her I'm going to call later.

Black- Okay. Let me speak to Lily again.

Uncle Sam gave the phone to Lily.

Lily- Hello?

Black- You have a great time, okay?

Lily- Okay. I love you.

Black- I love you, too. Take care.

I waited until I heard Lily hang up then I hung up after her. I began stretching. I was so happy to hear from her because it made my day feel much better. Just as I began thinking what was I going to do the doorbell rang so I put on my bedroom slippers and headed downstairs then opened the door.

Blue- Are you sleeping?

Black- No. I just woke up. Are you mad at me?

Blue- Actually, I love you more than ever. (She gave Black a hug, then released.)

Black- Come in.

I was so happy that she was not mad at me. I closed the door behind her.

Blue- (sitting on the couch) So what do you have planned for today?

Black- To tell you the truth, without doing a job I'm kind of bored.

Blue- Well, do you want to go to Virginia?

Black- Virginia. What's in Virginia?

Blue- Look, do you want to come?

Black- You better not do anything off the wall. Let me take a shower.

The highway was the way to life, Thomas would say. In a strange type of manner I kind of believed him. I loved to travel and I hoped one day I would make it to a place so far that people would forget me. I glanced at Blue as her hair blew wildly from her car window as she drove. She was my best friend and it took so long to recognize it. She was the only person besides Judy and Lily that I trusted. Hours passed and we finally arrived. I was so surprised at what I saw that it brought a smile to my face. Naked women danced sexy on cars, cement, and others. It was like one big freaky party. No one had shame and that was the good thing about it. Blue must have known I've never been to this because I was really fascinated.

Black- Blue, you've been here before?

Blue- This was one of my best money-making blocks. What do you think? (She laughed.)

Black- (laughing) You're crazy.

We spent our whole day at that party. It was the best time that I had in a long time. As we headed back home it was dark. I almost forgot about having a date with Rodney so I had to drive fast. As I was getting dressed I could hear the doorbell ring. I was really starting to hate that bell. Butterflies swarmed around in my stomach as Judy opened the door.

Judy- (surprised) Rodney, how are you?

Rodney- Fine, and you? (He gave Judy a kiss on the cheek.)

Judy- Fine. You look great. I'll call her down for you. Black!

Black- I'll be right down.

I was so nervous that my heart jumped out of my chest. I walked downstairs to greet Rodney. He watched me as if I were a supermodel. I couldn't help but to blush.

Judy- Oh, honey, don't you just look beautiful.
Black- (smiling) Thank you. (She looked at Rodney.) Ready?

As I sat in Rodney's car nothing but memories flashed back to the day we came back from Dorney Park. They all were so mad at me. I looked at him with a sad face.

Black- (with a puppy face) Sorry about your car, Rodney. I'm glad you got it fixed.
Rodney- (laughing) It's cool. Boy, if I could find that person who did it I would shake the hell out of them. Possibly choke them.
Black- Shit. That never happened before. That was a first.
Rodney- That was a last because I'm not parking my car by your house again.

I laughed because Rodney had a great sense of humor. If I wasn't mistaken he was the perfect guy for me. It took us half an hour to get to his house. I never would have imagined in a million years him living in the house that he did. His house was so amazing that it could have been mistaken for a woman's house. I was so impressed, though I didn't see how he did it. Personally I didn't think you could afford it on Federal Express income.

Black- Rodney, what is it you do for a living?
Rodney- Well, being that I don't have a family I'm able to work two jobs Monday through Friday. I work for Federal Express and on the weekend I do construction. I have to save every dime I get.

I still didn't see how he did it. My mom always said that men were neater than women and boy, was she right.

Black- You don't get lonely at times? I mean you're all alone in this big house.

Rodney- A lot of times I get lonely, so I just go outside. There's plenty of action in the city. Would you like some wine? I have white, peach, or red.

Black- Red is fine. Thank you.

Rodney- Are you hungry? I could cook for you.

Black- No thanks, I'm full from all the food I ate in Virginia.

Rodney- Oh, you went to Virginia today.

Black- Yeah. Blue and I went today. She took me to a big freak festival. I loved it.

Rodney- A freak festival?

Black- You know, nude, sex, and wildness.

Rodney handed me my drink.

Rodney- You actually went there?

Black- Yeah.

Rodney- Wow, so you like to travel?

Black- I love to travel. One day I'd like to move to Florida or Mexico.

Rodney- Why so far?

Black- To get away. To be free.

Rodney- You are free.

Black- (weak smile) I know.

Rodney- What exactly do you do for a living? You have a beautiful home, nice jeep, and you're still a baby.

Black- Baby! No. Well, maybe I am a baby but I've lived my life like a grownup. When my family died I inherited a lot of money because I was the only one to survive. That was years ago and feels like yesterday.

Rodney- Sorry to hear about that and your friend.

Black- It's okay. They're all in a better place.

Rodney- So do you plan to have any more children?

Black- No, it's just me and Lily.

Rodney- I would love to meet her.

Black- Well, on her first day back I'll bring her by. She'll be back in two weeks. She's having a great time at Disney World.

Rodney- Lucky her.

Black- (smiling) Yeah.

Our conversation went on for hours. In fact, we talked ourselves until we became tired. The wine had me feeling sexy. I wanted to kiss Rodney so bad but I didn't have the slightest clue what to do. I looked at him and he was already staring at me. I found myself losing control as I looked at his lips. God, I wanted to kiss him. Finally he leaned over and kissed me. Though I had no idea what I was doing I kissed back. The kisses moved down my neck, down my chest and into my shirt. I became nervous so I stopped him.

Black- Look, Rodney, I....

Rodney- It's okay, let's go to bed.

The next morning I woke up to breakfast in bed. Rodney had cooked up the place and man was he a great cook. That was very impressive in a man. Meanwhile, Lt. Franks walked out his office.

Detective Cargo- Lt. Franks, may I have a word with you? (He flagged Lt. Franks.)

Lt. Franks walked over to Detective Cargo's desk.

Lt. Franks- You were just the person I was looking for.

Detective Cargo- What's up?

Lt. Franks- I need you to get a printout on the robbery at the Leer building. I think we have a match.

Detective Cargo- Oh yeah, on what? Mr. Mann and the Leer building?

Lt. Franks- How'd you know?

Detective Cargo- I've been working extra hard on this case. I'm trying to do some serious damage.

Lt. Franks- That's great. You know, Detective, sometimes if you go to a scenery by yourself you get a lot of work done. You might even find something you overlooked.

Detective Cargo took Lt. Franks' advice and went back to the scenery at the Leer building. He began looking around for clues. He searched for seconds, minutes, even hours. Then he came across the red paint on the fire escape.

Detective Cargo- Well, well, well. What do we have here?

Who else drove that red Acura but Pink. It was bad enough that detective had our names and addresses now he really had a reason to bother us. The following morning he decided to pay her a little visit. He banged so rudely on the door that she became furious.

Pink- (opening the door) Do you have a problem with knocking, Detective?

Detective Cargo- This is an extremely big house with no doorbell. That's hard to believe.

Pink- (aggravated) What do you want? Oh yeah, I received your note you left me. I'm not a big fan on words.

Detective Cargo- (smiling) Do you drive a red Acura?

Pink- Yes, I do.

Detective Cargo- I see. Well, where is it?

Pink- It's in the shop.

Detective Cargo- Why is it in the shop?

Pink- What is this, a survey?

Detective Cargo- No, I just want to know why.

Pink- For rim repair and a regular checkup.

Detective Cargo- Okay, well, can you tell me, how close were you and Grey Prescott?

Pink- Pretty close, she was a good friend of mine. Why do you ask?

Detective Cargo- Well, because it's my job.

Pink- Well, Detective, I'm pretty tired of your face so if you want to know what shop my car is in it's at John's Auto Shop. Have a nice day. (She closed the door rudely in the detective's face.)

Detective Cargo walked away, got into his car and headed for the shop. Pink just watched him from behind her blinds. She really did put the car in the shop. After Thomas spotted after the job he advised her to put it in the shop. He even told her to pay the mechanic extra to keep hush on the paint job. Detective Cargo arrived at the shop and walked inside. Different types of cars were being worked on by several different mechanics. He walked to the back searching for Pink's car without asking for help. Finally he found it. He began observing the car to see if it had any scrapes. He walked to the back of the car and still found nothing. One of the mechanics spotted him and started walking toward him.

Mechanic- Hey, what are you doing back there? You have no business back there.

Detective Cargo- (getting out his badge) I'm a detective. (He held up his badge.) Do you know who owns this car?

Mechanic- I know it belongs to some lady.

Detective Cargo- You wouldn't know her name, right?

Mechanic- No, I don't. Not by heart.

Detective Cargo- What was done to the car?

Mechanic- Rim repair and a regular checkup.

Detective Cargo- Is there any chance I could look inside the car?

Mechanic- Do you have a search warrant?

Detective Cargo- No, I don't.

Mechanic- Well, in that case, no, you can't.

Detective Cargo- (smiling) Thanks for your time.

Detective Cargo walked away so mad you could see steam rising from his head. I decided to take a shower at Rodney's house then go home to change my clothes. I promised him I would reunite with him later in the week. After I got dressed I went to Judy room to look for her but she wasn't there so I decided to go and pay Grey some respect. On my way to the graveyard I stopped at a gas station and bought some fresh flowers and tissue. It took me a while to find her grave but soon the search ceased. I sat down on her grave and placed the new flowers on top of the old.

Black- (crying) Hi, baby. I miss you so much. You're lucky you can't hear me curse you out and you know why. Why didn't you tell me you were pregnant? You know I was a good friend and you can tell me anything. Is that why you wanted to move away, to start you a family, and not have to worry about this bullshit anymore? Right now I'm so confused that I don't know who to trust. This group fell completely apart since you died. Nothing's the same and I'm getting worried. I don't even care for Pink or Red anymore. They're becoming wicked just like Thomas. I'm ready to get out of this life that I'm in so I can be there for Lily. I really can't picture your wild ass with children. We most certainly don't want them to pick our bad habits. (She laughed.) Girl, Rodney, do you remember him from the diner that time? Well, he and I have been doing the couple thing lately. I like him more than I thought I would ever like any man. Terrance, he's happy with Samantha. I still hate him for doing that to me. Lily, she's doing just fine....

Suddenly I heard a noise come from the bushes so I stood up. I then pulled out my gun before I began walking toward the bushes.

Black- Who's there? Who's there?

No one answered so I walked even closer to the bushes. Just as I was three feet away Thomas came from out the bushes. The gun was directly in his face.

> Thomas- Get that damn gun out of my face. What are you, stupid?
> Black- (removing the gun) Oh, I'm sorry, I didn't mean to scare you.
> Thomas- Scare, girl, do you know who I am?
> Black- I apologize. How long have you been there?
> Thomas- Long enough and that's all that matters.

I prayed Thomas didn't hear what I said because that was the last thing I needed.

> Black- If you're looking for the grave it's....
> Thomas- I know where it is. I'm smarter than you.
> Black- Sorry. I'll talk to you later.
> Thomas- Hold on, I want you to gather everyone for a meeting tomorrow. I have another job and it will be at night. I'll discuss everything tomorrow. As you know it's time for the Jumble.
> Black- Oh, hell, it came fast.

The Jumble was where several big-time bosses would gather together and order famous chefs to cook for them, gamble, bet on female mud wrestlers, and trade men. They had these gatherings once every year toward the end of the summer.

> Thomas- Yes, it did, so just tell everyone to be prepared.
> Black- Alright. Will the men be there?
> Thomas- Who?
> Black- You know, Leach, Mike, Cam, and Dre. Will they be there?
> Thomas- Oh yeah, they'll be there.

For some reason I didn't believe him.

Black- Okay. Talk to you later.

As I walked away Thomas gave me the cruelest look anyone could give. Meanwhile, Blue was cooking spaghetti. She was basically finished when her phone rang.

Blue- (picking it up) Hello?
Voice- Hi, bitch, fuck your man lately? I know I did.
Blue- Who is this?
Voice- Who do you want it to be? You're so stupid and pathetic. I can't believe Felix loves a hoe. Bet you won't dare wear a tank top.
Blue- (crying) Fuck you!

Blue hung up the phone and began crying even harder. She was so tired of those phone calls that it was ridiculous. Felix was messing around because that person knew too much information. Then the phone rang again, so she let it ring four times before she picked it up.

Blue- Listen, you sick bitch, if you call my house one more time I'll put two in your head, I promise.
Black- Why do you want to do that to me? What did I do?
Blue- Black. Oh, girl, I'm sorry.
Black- Still getting those phone calls, huh?
Blue- I just received one before you called.
Black- Are you okay?
Blue- I guess so. What are you doing?
Black- Judy just called and reminded me about the cookout today. Want to come? Plus we have a meeting tomorrow.
Blue- Come and get me.

I picked Blue up and headed to my house. One thing everyone loved was Judy's cookouts. As we pulled up the hill we noticed several cars already parked outside.

Blue- Is this all your family?

Black- Yeah, friends also. Judy said you can always buy friendship with food.

Blue- (laughing) She's right.

I parked the car then we went to the backyard where the cookout took place. As we walked over to the pool I spotted Isles on the grill.

Black- (turning around to Blue) Look, if you want to go back home I'll understand. I don't want you to get in any more trouble.

Blue- What are you talking about? Is something wrong?

Black- Isles is cooking on the grill. I didn't know he was coming.

Blue- No, I don't want to go home. He just makes the cookout even better.

Isles looked up and spotted us then waved with the big fork. I wondered, was he still mad at me about his car?

Black- You want something to drink?

Blue- Not Kool-Aid.

Black- Duh, of course. Go talk to Isles. I'll be right back. (She walked away.)

Blue- (walking up to Isles) So who decided to make you chef man of burn?

Isles- (laughing) Oh, so you got jokes. I'd love to see you sweat over this grill.

Blue- You know I look best when I sweat.

Judy was in the kitchen cooking as I walked in.

Black- Where were you when I came by here earlier?

Judy- I had to pick up some things for the cookout and to have another key made. I can't find mine. Have you seen it?

Black- No.

Judy- Well, honey, you can tell me about your little date later. I have some guests to entertain. (She kissed Black on the cheek.)

I gathered several beers and headed back to the cookout. Blue and Isles were still talking so I had to interrupt them.

Black- (handing a beer to Blue) Here you go. (She handed a beer to Isles.) Here you go. I'll be on the back balcony. (She walked away.)

Minutes later Blue and Isles joined me.

Black- Isles, are you mad at me about your car?

Isles- I was but I'm not anymore.

Black- I knew you were.

Isles- So Blue, did your man beat you?

Blue- (mad) That's not funny, Isles.

Isles- Hey, it was only a joke. I'm sorry.

Black- (switching the subject) So Isles, why are you still being bothered with Thomas? Why don't you stay out while you can?

Isles- (sipping his beer) Thomas owes me a lot of money.

Black- How much?

Isles- He owes me three million.

Blue- Damn, why so much?

Isles- Well, on that last job we did it was for twenty-four million in diamonds. You remember? He was supposed to give me three million dollars but of course I never saw a penny of that money. He didn't even care I went to jail. I've been nagging him about my money for a while now and I'm getting fed up. You know what? I haven't seen the group I was training since I got here.

Blue- We've been asking him that for weeks now.

Black- I saw him today when I was visiting Grey.

Blue- Visiting?

Black- Yeah.

Isles- That's strange. Thomas has been around me all my life and he's never visited any of the men that died.

Black- I thought it was weird, too. Maybe he does miss her.

Blue- Yeah, like a tree on a highway.

It was strange, though. The way Thomas was coming from out of those bushes was like he was trying to hide.

Black- We have another job to do tomorrow.

Blue- What time?

Black- Forgot to ask. I'll call him tonight and ask. I'll let you know.

Isles- Well, make sure you tell me so I can be there to ask for my money.

The following morning we met at the bowling alley on Larks Road. As usual Thomas was in a bad mood. He cursed, eyed, and spit so much I thought he was going insane. Red and Pink pretended to be on top. They didn't even say hello. Thomas didn't care how we felt about each other anymore. All he cared about was his money and ways.

Thomas- Well, as you all know it's about that time to join the Jumble. I'm just letting you know ahead of time so that you can be prepared. We're not going to make that an issue today because we have a job tomorrow night.

After the meeting Blue followed me home in her car. She was really on my tail as if something was terribly wrong. Maybe she got another one of those phone calls. As we pulled up in front of my house she met me as I was getting out my car.

Blue- Did you see those bitches today? They didn't say a word to us. Who the fuck do they or Thomas think they are?

Black- I don't know but we can't let that bother us right now.

Blue- Black, we have a job tomorrow. Who's to say nothing will go wrong? Last time you almost got shot.

Black- You still think Pink tried to kill me, huh?

Blue- Shit, she tried without doing it herself. What's wrong with you, why won't you believe me?

In a way I kind of did believe her it just was that it didn't sound right. I didn't know what to say so I just looked at her.

Black- Come on, girl, let's go get a drink.

Blue- I really do need one. (She walked into Black's house.)

When we entered the house Isles was in the living room sitting on the couch, waiting for me.

Black- (closing the door) Oh, Isles, I forgot to call you and let you know where we were meeting.

Isles- I know. I'm mad at you.

Black- Oh, please don't be like that. Please. Come have a drink with Blue and me.

We drank so much that it was daytime when we started and dark when we finished. We were completely drunk.

Isles- Talk to me, girls.

Blue- Earlier I was telling Black that the Wicked Witch of the West tried to kill her.

We all laughed for about fifteen seconds.

Black- Maybe they are.

Isles- Who you talking about?

Blue- Pink. Her and Red are becoming Thomas' daughters.

Isles- Are you serious?

Blue- I'm serious as a bad weave. It's like ever since Grey died they changed.

Isles- Well, maybe they miss her.

Blue- We all miss her, that's not a reason to change toward your friends.

Black- Did you know she was pregnant when she died?

Isles- (shocked) What?

Blue- (surprised) What?

Black- Yeah, that detective told me. Her and her baby is in a better place. At least she's away from Thomas and his bullshit.

Blue- I know but it's just that whoever killed her didn't know she was pregnant, or they didn't care.

Isles- Don't worry. They'll have their day with the big man upstairs.

Blue- Amen.

Black- I just wonder, why was she walking instead of taking her car?

Blue- Remember she rode in with Pink and Red that day. Remember you took me to get my car and her car was still at the spot.

Black- That's right. Did they ever say where they dropped her off?

Blue- I never asked.

Black- (thinking) Well, I'm going to make sure I ask.

Isles- I hope they made sure she was alright.

Blue- (intoxicated) Oh God, I'm so drunk. (She stood up.) Girl, I'm staying at your housed tonight, unless you have something to do. (She nearly fell.)

Black- (catching Blue) Girl, don't be silly. Go lay down.

Blue- Goodnight, Isles.

Isles- Goodnight, Blue.

Isles watched Blue stumble up the stairs. She was so drunk that it was more like a struggle for her. Finally she made it.

Black- You still love her, huh?

Isles- I'll love her always and forever. I don't know why she stopped writing me. Women can only take but so much when a man's in jail. I wish I never would have gone but I had no control over it. If I didn't have that good-ass lawyer I would have done a lot more time than six years for two bodies. I would never put her through that again. She's a married woman now, she doesn't want me anymore.

Black- Don't say that.

Isles- (standing up) It's true. May I use your bathroom?

Black- Yeah. It's upstairs to your right.

I felt bad because I knew that Blue and Isles wanted to be together. Meanwhile, Isles was walking upstairs for the bathroom. He turned right and walked toward it then pushed the door in. There he saw Blue's entire body covered in black-and-blue marks. She turned around quickly and slammed the door in his face. Isles stood back in shock and disbelief. That's why she got mad when he made that joke about Felix beating her. He really did. Four seconds later she opened the bathroom door back open.

Blue- (furious) Do you have a problem with knocking? Are you stupid or something? Why didn't....

Isles- You let him do that to your body?

She just stared at him while she was ashamed and embarrassed.

Blue- Look, just mind your business. This has nothing to do with you.

Isles- Did I ever put my hands on you? Did I?

Blue- (hesitating, then crying) No.

Isles- So, why are you letting him? You're either going to be lied up in some hospital bed or casket. What the fuck do you think you got guns for? Did you forget how to use it?

Blue- Look, just mind your business.

Isles- (loud) You are my business!

Isles was so loud that Judy woke from her sleep as I hurried up the stairs.

Blue- I swear, you better not mention this to Black or I'll never speak to you again.

He loved Blue more than anything so her not speaking to him would kill him. He was puzzled but more be lowered than anything. If he would have not gone to jail in the first place, then none of this would have ever happened. Judy opened her door and came out her room.

Judy- Is everything okay?
Black- (reaching the top of the stairs) I don't know. (She looked at Isles and Blue.) What's going on?

He just stared hard at Blue as tears rushed down his face. I couldn't believe that Isles was crying.

Judy- Isles, are you okay?
Black- (touching Isles on the shoulder) What's wrong? Blue, what you do to him?

Blue put her head down and stared at the floor. Whatever it was had her to ashamed to look at us.

Isles- (wiping away his tears) Look, Black, I'll be seeing you later. (He walked away.)

Blue still continued to look at the floor as he walked down the stairs then out the door.

Black- Blue, you're not going to tell me what's going on?

Blue- Leave me alone. (She ran into the guest room, then slammed the door)

Judy and I just looked at each other then shrugged our shoulders.

Black- Ma, can I talk to you for a minute?
Judy- Sure, step in my office.

I walked in her room then she shut the door behind me.

Judy-So what's up, honey?
Black- (taking a deep inhale) Where should I start? It's like everyone's changing.
Judy- Changing? Are you talking about me?
Black- No, I'm talking about Thomas, Pink, Red. Grey's gone forever and Blue's hiding things from me. I feel like I can't trust anyone anymore. I don't even know how I got into this business.
Judy- Well, who's Thomas and what business are you talking about?
Black- (smiling) Did I say business?
Judy- Yes, you did. Is there something you want to tell me?
Black- I have so much to tell you. First of all, I want to know how come you never questioned me where I was going or what I did for a living.
Judy- I guess because you're a strong, independent woman.
Black- You've been letting me do whatever I wanted since you took me in.
Judy- You know, I'm going to stop beating it around the bush. From what's happened to you in your past you deserve whatever you want. I'm not saying I pity you for what's happened but you finished school, stayed out of trouble. If there was trouble I didn't know about it. You're cautious. You never kept me worried about what you were doing or if you were alive. I know what you do.
Black- What are you talking about?

Judy- Black, what I'm about to tell you, is something you must keep to yourself except when the time is right. I know what you do for a living. You see, my sister Kathy used to be in the same work for the same man that murdered you're family. The day he killed you're family she was at my house. She already knew what was going to happen, and so did your dad. They were so close that they never kept any secrets from each other. Your mom was quite jealous of them and almost left your dad because of her. The day that Zane Passage disappeared my sister paid me $86,000 to take you in. She would have done so herself but Zane was also after her, so she had to move away and change her identity. (She was crying/) She told me that I would save your life and be thankful in the end. You've grown to be a beautiful woman and I would have taken you in even if she didn't give me that money. I'm sorry that I have to tell you this but it's necessary. Listen, when the time is right you'll meet Kathy and then you take it from there.

I became so confused and angry at the same time. I couldn't believe what Judy was saying to me. This situation was becoming more and more difficult for me. Judy was crying so hard that I had to give her a hug to let her know it was alright. Man, there was so much that I wanted to know. When would the time be right?

Judy- I really don't care what you do for a living because you take care of Lily, yourself, and me. That's what you call a real woman. You have everything that you need. What more could you ask for?
Black- A man.
Judy- (laughing) You do have one.
Black- Rodney is not my man.
Judy- Who said I was talking about Rodney? Did you enjoy your date?
Black- Yes, I enjoyed myself a lot. I like him.

Judy became motionless and put her head down.

Black- What's wrong, Ma?

Judy- (picking her head up) I fear for Terrance.

Black- Why's that?

Judy- Did you see the way she looked at me when I told her to help with the table?

Black- Like her whole world shut down.

Judy- I just feel like if I wanted a man to be happy I would have to get along with his mother. It was like she didn't care. I know he's with the wrong woman. Remember a mother knows, just like I know the two of you love each other.

Black- (feeling embarrassed) What?

Judy- You heard me. I know that the two of you loved each other for a long time now. That day when he told me you were hurt killed me. He said to me, "Ma, don't let her die. I love her."

Black- (emotional) He said that?

Judy- Yes, he did and I believed him. I know he does.

Black- I mean that makes me feel good and all but (standing up) he's getting married. I'm tired so I'll talk to you later. Goodnight.

I walked over and opened her bedroom door.

Judy- Black.

I turned around.

Judy- Never give up. Take what's yours.

Black- How?

Judy- God will make a way good or bad. In the end you'll understand why he did the bad things for the good. Goodnight and I love you. (She was smiling.)

Black- I love you, too. (She was smiling.)

The following night seemed to take forever. Blue stayed over the whole day at my house so that we could go to the job together. I didn't even stress her on last night with her and Isles because whatever it was had to be bad if he was crying. Blue and I stepped out of my jeep and walked over to Thomas, Red, and Pink. I was surprised because he never came with us to any night jobs, so this was a first.

Thomas- Everything good?

Black- (confused) Yeah.

Pink- What's up, Blue?

Blue- (confused) What's up?

Red- We're going to grab a bite after the job. Want to come?

Black- Yeah, I'm starving.

Blue- I'll catch up to you later. (She looked at Black.) I have so much to do.

Thomas- Okay. This building has cameras. What I want you to do is collect all jewelry and money from the ninth floor up. That's where all the rich people live. Security guards are going to start their routine check from the first floor in five minutes. You know the deal put all the people in the closets, don't shoot unless someone's trying to kill you. Room 412 is Warren Owens' room. He's loaded so take everything in sight. Plus he's got a safe in his room and I don't know the combination so you'll have to blow it. That's your job, Red. Get in, get out. Last thing the way to exit is the top floor fire escape. I'll be down there with the car started.

Black- What about my car?

Thomas- I'll start it for you. It'll be right behind my car. Red and Pink, you take the right elevator, and Blue and Black, you two take the left. No one is to go to the next floor without anyone. We have two minutes so take the elevators to the ninth floor and began at nine o'clock.

Blue- You didn't tell us how many floors there are.

Thomas- (laughing) I did forget that, huh? There are fifteen floors, now go.

God only knew why everyone was in such a good mood but I wasn't complaining. It felt rather good. Blue and I entered the elevator on the left as Red and Pink entered on the right. When the elevator doors closed Blue leaned over and gave me a hug so hard I thought she was leaving.

Black- What was that for?
Blue- What's it for, just be careful.

I really had no idea what she was thinking. Was it the worst? I became a little uncomfortable and took a deep breath as I rubbed my forehead. I looked her before the elevator doors opened then shook my head. Soon the time had come. Blue stepped out and sprayed every camera that she saw then we began. We kicked in doors of all the people that resided in the hotel and began robbing them for their goods. Red and Pink seemed to be much faster at the job than Blue and I. They waited for us at the exit to the next flight of stairs. We flew through the floors so fast that before I knew it we were on the fifteenth floor. We were hustling our ass off. I've never seen us work or sweat harder than the men.

Red- I'm going to Mr. Owens' room. Cover me.

Pink did so while Blue and I finished up the other rooms. Red ran and kicked in his room door. His eyes grew wide as he saw them with their guns.

Warren- Don't kill me, please.

Just then a woman walked out the bathroom to see what was going on, and screamed once she saw Red with the gun. Red smacked her so hard that she fell to the floor. She then put her gun on the bed and went to attach the bomb on his safe. Pink shoved Mr. Owens and the woman in the closet as Blue and I walked in the room.

Red- (running) Everyone, get out, it's going to blow!

We all ran out the room, stood back while it blew, then hurried back inside so we could collect his property. Red ran over and picked up a small leather pouch from the safe and opened it. It was full of diamonds so she put it inside the bag along with his watches, jewelry, and money.

Pink- Come on, let's go. Let's get out of here.

We all ran for the roof. My heart pounded as if I were about to lose control. We could hear sirens so that meant security had reached the ninth floor.

Pink- I see the ladder. (She ran toward the ladder.)

We all ran for the ladder.

Red- (stop running) Oh, shit, oh God, I forgot the gun on Mr. Owens' bed.

We stopped running and began to become worried.

Black- What the fuck? Where is it?
Red- On his bed, please, Black, you got to go get it. I got to get these diamonds to Thomas or else. You know.
Black- (running back) Alright, go ahead. I'm coming right behind you.
Red- Hurry up.

I hurried up and ran back into the building. I had to be quick and careful because trouble was on its way. Meanwhile, Red, Pink, and Blue ran to the ladder. Red went down first.

Thomas- Hurry up, let's go, they're almost here.

Red made it down safely and went inside the car. Pink went to the ladder and put one foot on it then turned to Blue.

> Blue- Hurry up and go down!
> Pink- You always thought you were better than me.
> Blue- What? (She was confused.)

Just then Pink pointed her gun at Blue and shot her once in the chest. Blue fell motionless to the ground. Pink hurried up down the fire escape then into the car with Thomas behind her. They pulled off and didn't think twice about looking back. I could hear a gunshot go off from Mr. Owens' room. Instantly I became nervous and worried. I began to breathe funny. As I ran to the roof with two guns in my hand I spotted Blue lying in a pool of blood, hardly breathing. I became so scared I didn't know what to do.

> Black- Blue! Blue! (She ran to Blue.) Oh my God, what happened? Thomas! Thomas!

When Thomas didn't answer I ran to the fire escape and looked down. A tear came down my face once I saw that he wasn't down there. He didn't even move my car behind his like he said he was going to do. They left us. I came back to reality as I heard sirens. I had to think of something quick. I ran back over to Blue and looked at her. She lay there with her eyes closed and her gun in her hand. What was I going to do with these three guns? As I put my hand up to my forehead I spotted an industrial furnish. I took her gun from out her hand and ran to it. I tossed all three guns down it then took my top shirt off. I ran back over to Blue and picked her up then wiped the blood from underneath her with my shirt. I then dragged her back into Mr. Owens' room, laid her on the floor, and went back and retraced any blood I didn't get. When I was finished I threw the shirt down it also. I ran back into Mr. Owens' room and closed the door, then let him and the woman out the closet.

> Black- Mr. Owens, please, please help us. My friend's been shot and

she's going to die if you don't help us.

Warren- First you rob me, now you want me to help you, fuck you.

Black- No, Mr. Owens, look, we were sent to rob you. I didn't know that it was going to turn out like this or I would have never done it. Look, if you help me I will give you the man that sent us, give you everything he took from you, plus interest. All you have to do is help us. Please, I swear to you. I give you my word along with my life. Just help me, help her (looking at Blue), please.

Warren- I don't know if....

Black- Look, if you're going to do it we have to hurry. The cops are on their way up.

Warren- Okay, but you better not fuck me around or you'll be as dead as I want you.

Black- I promise. I give you my word.

Warren- You know people did see you rob them. How are you going to get out of here without someone seeing you?

Black- I have a plan.

Meanwhile, Detective Cargo was in the building, exiting people from their rooms. He was highly upset due to the fact that this wasn't the only robbery in this month. He soon reached the fifteenth floor and spotted Mr. Owens pacing the floor.

Warren- Help me, my friend has been shot. She's badly hurt. I need help.

Detective Cargo ran for the room with a couple of first-aid people behind him. When he entered the room he saw me on the floor in a bloody shirt holding Blue while she nearly bled to death.

Detective Cargo- Okay, people, let's move!

Meanwhile, back at the house, Judy was taking a very hot comfortable bath. She was so exhausted and full that she just knew she would fall asleep afterwards. Her bubbles were so high in her water that it nearly overflowed. Suddenly she heard some noise so she jumped up put her bathrobe on and headed downstairs. She walked through the house checking for about three minutes but found nothing. She began to feel a cool drift so she went to the back door and found that it was open. She became very paranoid.

Judy- Black, is that you?

No one replied so she took a look out the door.

Judy- Black, is that you?

Still no one replied so she closed the door, locked it and headed back upstairs. She closed the bathroom door and took off her bathrobe. Once again she would try to enjoy her comfortable bath. Just as soon as she put one foot in the tube she began to fry. Someone had put a hairdryer in the tub. The only reason why she didn't notice it was because of the bubbles covering the wire. She had stepped into her death. Finally it was over as she lay dead floating in a tube of water. Due to Mr. Owens being a very popular and wealthy man we were able to get escorted to the hospital before anyone. We even beat the press. Detective Cargo decided to question Mr. Owens in private.

Detective Cargo- Okay, do you mind running this by me again? What happened?
Warren- Well, I was in the room watching television.
Detective Cargo- Who?
Warren- The girls and I. When all of a sudden two men kicked in my door and pointed their guns at us. Blue tried to run so that's when one of them shot her in her in the chest. Then the other man shoved me and my other two friends in the closet. They were searching for something then ran to the roof. We were too afraid to go for help so we just stayed behind with Blue. I think there were more of them, I'm not sure.

Detective Cargo- Okay, one more question. What were all of you doing in the room, and did they take anything?

Warren- Oh, the ladies are strippers and the only thing that was stolen from me was five hundred dollars and it was for the ladies.

Detective Cargo- Thank you. Have a good night and be careful.

Detective Cargo was still curious because he just couldn't figure it out. Just then his dispatcher went off.

Radio- Detective Cargo, we have a 187 at Danbury Avenue.

 Detective Cargo walked over and picked up his dispatcher.

Detective Cargo- What's that?

Radio- I said we have a 187 at Danbury Avenue.

Detective Cargo- What number?

Radio- 411.

Detective Cargo- Give me ten minutes.

Detective Cargo felt jumpy because that code meant death. He also knew that was my house address. He jumped in his car and drove dangerously getting there. As he drove up several police cars and a coroner were parked outside of my house. As Detective Cargo walked into my house, Lt. Franks met up with him.

Lt. Franks- I've been waiting for you.

Detective Cargo- I was questioning a victim at a robbery.

Lt. Franks- Did you get far?

Detective Cargo- Actually I have a lot of work to do. (He grabbed latex gloves.) What do we have?

Lt. Franks- Female, age forty-four. Her name is Judy Watson. She was killed from a hairdryer falling in her tub water. I predict it was an accident.

Detective Cargo felt horrible. Especially for me because I was losing everyone close to me. It was bad enough I was at the hospital with one friend and now

I would have to attend a funeral for my second mother. His heart fell out of his chest as he headed into the bathroom. They had already taken her out of the tube and covered her. After Detective Cargo bent down and pulled the sheet off her he turned his head quickly. He remained silent for five seconds.

Detective Cargo- Was anyone in the house when this happened?
Lt. Franks- No, we received a phone call saying someone heard screaming from the house. There are footprints from the bathroom to the back door so she might have heard something.
Detective Cargo- Did you contact any of her family members?
Lt. Franks- Yeah, we contacted her son Terrance Watson. He'll be at the hospital to review the body. He's really no good right now.
Detective Cargo- Yeah….

Suddenly Judy jumped up screaming. It scared Detective Cargo so bad that he fell backwards to the floor.

Detective Cargo- Oh, shit. I thought you said she was dead.
Coroner #1- I know she was. (He backed up.)
Coroner #2- I could have sworn. (He backed up.)
Lt. Franks- Get her to a hospital! Move! Move!

Detective Cargo followed the ambulance to the hospital. He rubbed his neck due to the adventurous night he was having. Blue and I had just arrived at the hospital. I tried calling Felix but he wasn't there so the best that I could do was Isles. He seemed devastated and began crying over the phone immediately. When he arrived at the hospital his eyes were so puffy and red that I gave him an enormous hug.

Isles- She has to make it. She just has to.
Black- She will just stay strong.
Isles- What happened?
Black- You know what, Isles, we're going to save this all for tomorrow.

Okay?

Isles- (crying) Okay. I'm going to go and wait in the waiting room until further notice. (He walked to the waiting room.)

Black- I'm going to call Judy. I know she's worried.

I found it very unusual that Judy didn't answer the phone. I figured that she was in a very deep sleep. I hung the phone up and heard some awful screaming. The pitch of the voice assured me that it was a woman screaming. As I began walking toward the way of the screaming woman the voice became more and more familiar to me. Suddenly a team of doctors and nurses pushed Judy past me screaming to the top of her lungs. She kicked and screamed as the worked on her to try and keep her alive. It was hard to recognize her from her flesh being burned but I knew it was her.

Black- (scared) Oh my God.

I began running behind the stretcher calling for Judy. She just continued to scream. Isles ran out the visiting room and ran behind me. He hadn't a clue to what was going on. Terrance, Samantha, and Detective Cargo ran into the hospital and in the direction of the screaming voice. They were completely frightened and looked scared then ever. The team of doctors and nurses pushed Judy into the operating room and closed the door. I could still see them through the glass window. I blanked out and began losing my mind as I watched her yell at the top of her lungs. Just then Judy looked at me and took her last breath then died. Her line went dead as I began pulling my hair. The doctors tried to bring her back but it was useless. This time she was dead for real. I picked a chair up and tried to throw it through the glass window but it wouldn't break. The team of doctors and nurse became frightened and ran out the operating room. I picked up another chair and tried to throw it but Terrance had taken it from me. He then put the chair down and hugged me until I calmed down. We both fell to our knees in tears and hugged one another. I could feel tears dropping on my face so I looked at him and hugged him even tighter.

Detective Cargo- Get her out of here, she's had enough.

Isles became so worried that he went back into the waiting room crying and praying for Blue to make it.

Samantha- Terrance, that's what I'm here for to hold you. Now let go of her.
Terrance- What did you say?
Samantha- I said I'm your wife so I should be holding you. Let her go.

Terrance could feel me trying to get up so he held me down even tighter.

Terrance- I think you better meet me at the house.
Samantha- No. You can meet me at the house but I won't be there. (She walked away.)

I continued to cry because basically my whole world shut down. All I could picture was her burnt flesh screaming at the top of her lungs. It was just awful. What was I going to tell Uncle Sam and Lily? Detective Cargo put his head down and blinked hard. He was completely off track.

Detective Cargo- You know what, Terrance? You should take her home and let her get some rest. Her friend was just shot about an hour ago and they don't know if she's going to make it. I'll be over tomorrow or the next day to ask her some questions.
Terrance- (shaking Detective Cargo's hand) Thank you.

Twenty minutes later Terrance walked me to his car and put me inside. I knew that a big part of our life had died and we would never get it back. I didn't realize that we pulled up in front of my house until I looked up. Once I realized where I was I got out of the car and started running. Terrance got out the car and chased me. Finally he caught me and held me tight.

Black- How could you bring me back to this stupid house? I hate this house.

Terrance- Black, this is your house, you can't hate it.

Black- Judy is gone, so this isn't my house. Why are you here?

Terrance- Please calm down. (He was crying.) I miss her too, but it's not going to bring her back. She's in a better place.

Black- Oh, God, what do I have to live for?

Terrance- Lily...and me.

I looked up and hoped I wasn't hearing things.

Black- What did you say?

Terrance- I said, "I love you, girl. I love you so much and I don't know how to let you go." (He was crying.) Do you know how it feels to love someone and watch them love someone in front of your face?

Black- Yes, I do.

Just then he kissed me. His smooth butter-like lips collided with mine. I hesitated as my stomach swarmed butterflies. All I wanted was to be with this man and here he was kissing me. He cuffed me in his arms as I began to kiss back. My body began to tremble.

Terrance- (whispering) Don't worry, I got you.

As our feelings exploded we found ourselves in my room on my bed. He began kissing my neck, which moved down into my shirt. He looked up at me and smiled.

Terrance- Are you ready?

Black- (still crying) More than ever.

My whole entire life was changing right in front of me. Slowly he took my shirt off and proceeded with sexy kisses over my breast. I gasped for air as his large fingers tickled my shoulders. Then he unsnapped my bra. My heart was beating so fast that it felt like a ball being bounced by a child. Slowly he took my bra down and began kissing my breasts. It felt weird but at the same time good. My nipples became aroused, pointy, and harder than ever, so he then sucked them. I arched my eyebrows. Terrance then unbuttoned my jeans and took them down. I just stood there in a thong while he observed my body. I felt so nude but appreciated. He stared at me while he undressed, then backed me up onto the bed. Once again he began kissing on my body so I just followed. Not because it made me look good but because it made me feel good. Once he removed my panties I began crying but held them back because this wasn't the place or time. He opened my legs and gave me something so new, so fresh that you do understand. I became a real woman. I did what I couldn't do and it was so perfect. I've never known something that can hurt so bad could feel so good. When it was over we lay in bed holding each other.

Black- Terrance.

Terrance- Yeah.

Black- I love you, too.

He smiled as we fell to sleep. The following day I woke up in the evening. As I began to stretch I could hear male voices coming from downstairs. I looked over and noticed Terrance was in the bed so one of the voices was his. I stood up out the bed, forgetting I was completely naked and hurried for my pajamas and bedroom slippers. I put them on and walked downstairs to the living room. Isles and Terrance sat there talking but stopped once they realized I was standing there.

Isles- How you doing, Black?

Black- I don't know how I feel. I'm just so confused. (She sat down on the couch next to Terrance.)

Terrance- (touching Black's leg) Everything's going to be just fine.

I looked at him remembering last night. It was so incredible that I wanted to marry him. Then I realized Judy's death wasn't a dream; it was real. I began to feel tears arriving so I just took a deep breath.

Terrance- You know what, Black? You owe me the truth on what's really going on. Why is there a detective after you? See, last night I thought he was just there because of my mother's death but he knows you and Blue. Are the two of you in trouble? You have to tell me something if you really love me, girl.

Black- Alright, look, I will tell you everything after I call Uncle Sam. He has to know, right? I know it's going to kill him. I don't want him to tell Lily. I want to tell her.

I hated every moment of speaking Judy's death to Uncle Sam. I've never heard him cry so hard in my life, but I couldn't help but to either. I just couldn't believe that she was gone. Terrance and Isles sat in the living room waiting impatiently for me to return.

Terrance- How is he?

Black- Horrible. They'll be here tomorrow at 12:40 in the morning. I have to get them from the airport; he's leaving his car.

Isles- You make any funeral arrangements?

Terrance- No, I'm waiting for the rest of the family to get up here then I'll do it. She has a policy, though, so we shouldn't have much to worry about. I know is funeral is going to be bad. I guess everyone went into the mute mode because we became quiet for a while.

Black- So Isles, how's Blue?

Isles- She went under and they removed the bullet. She was lucky because an inch more and she would have died. She's in critical condition right now. I have to go home and take a shower. I'll be back there later on.

Black- I'll stop by later on…. Isles, did she ever say who shot her?

Isles became quiet as if he didn't hear me. So I asked him again.

Black- Isles, did she say who shot her?

He just gave me this depressing look, but still kept quiet.

Black- Why the fuck won't you tell me who shot her? Tell me, damn it.
Isles- Pink.

Just then I ran to the table and grabbed Judy's car keys then headed out the door. I could hear Terrance calling me but I had things to find out. Like why didn't Thomas wait for us or pull out my car behind his? I felt bad I didn't listen to Blue. I was so stupid and blind that I could kick myself in my own ass.

Isles- (worried) Oh, no.
Terrance- Where's she going?
Isles- To find Pink.
Terrance- Isles, do you know what's going on?
Isles- Yeah, but I can't tell you.

I basically spent my whole afternoon looking for Thomas. Wherever he was I knew that Red and Pink would be with him. Around 4:15 I spotted his driver waiting for him outside of a Chinese buffet. I parked the car and got out then went inside. I began walking all over the restaurant until I saw them. When I saw them Pink was the only one that saw me.

Pink (whispering) Thomas, Black's here. I thought you said she would be in jail.
Thomas- Relax, don't get scared on me now.

I walked over to them with a look that could kill.

Black- Well, well, well. What the fuck is going on? That was some real bullshit you all were on last night. Is that why you were so nice? That's fucked up, Thomas, you left us.
Thomas- Have a seat.
Black- I'm not sitting down.

Thomas- Sit the fuck down now!

I hesitated at first but then I just sat down.

Thomas- If you ever, in your miserable life, talk to me like that again I'll kill you, bitch.

I became quiet and scared so I looked over to Red. She had her eyes closed with her head back as if she were asleep with a smile on her face.

Black- Pink, did you shoot Blue?
Pink- (pretending) Why, I'm shocked. I would never.

Thomas began to laugh as if it were a joke.

Black- Oh, so you think shit don't stink, huh?
Pink- Sure smells good to me.
Black- I'm glad you think so. Does anyone know that Judy was killed last night?
Pink- Well, I know she's happy to be away from you.

That little comment that she made made me so mad that I couldn't help but to smack her hard in her face. She just gave me this dirty look back and rubbed her cheek.

Black- (looking at Red) You don't have anything to say, Red?

Red picked her head up and opened her eyes.

Black- Do you have something to say?
Red- Yeah, what I have to say is….

Just then she began moaning. She moaned louder, harder, sexier. I had no idea why she was doing that. I thought she was losing her mind. Finally she had one last strong moan as Thomas and Pink started laughing. When she stopped she picked up a napkin from the table and held it. I became curious. Then Londa came from underneath the table. I became sick to my stomach once I realized she had just given Red oral sex under the table. She wiped her mouth with the napkin in Red's hand then looked at me.

Londa- Would you like some?

I picked up a fork from the table and put it to her neck.

Black- (holding the fork to Londa's neck) Would you like some?

Thomas grabbed my arm and dug his long sharp nails into it. He began digging so hard and deep that it became painful. My pride took over and encouraged me to continue to hold the fork against her neck. Once again he began digging even harder until I couldn't bear pain, so I just put the fork down on the table.

Thomas- The bathroom now! (He removed his nails from my arm.) Go.

I stormed off toward the bathroom as he followed behind me with his cane. I know he was mad but so was I. My life was becoming miserable and I didn't know why this was happening to me. Pink, Londa, and Red sat at the table with silly smirks on their faces. As I entered the bathroom my body began to shiver. I felt weak but awake. Once women realized Thomas was in the bathroom they began to stare at him.

Thomas- Alright, if you ever want to make children again I advise you to wipe your pussies and get it going.

One by one the women began to exit the bathroom as I stood there with my back turned. They looked exactly how I felt, terrified. Finally the last lady came out the stall and went out the door. When Thomas realized the bathroom was empty he picked his cane up and hit my directly on my back. I fell to the floor on my knees. A terrible pain shot from one end of my back to the other. I could feel tears pushing through my eyes but I held them back.

>Thomas- (taking a urine in the sink) I don't know what's come over you but personally I don't care. You were supposed to be in jail and Blue was supposed to be dead. If you know what's good for you, you'll shut your mouth and wait to see what I decide to do with you.
>
>Black- You know what? I think your mother dropped you on your head when you was a baby. You need some help, you sick mother....

I couldn't get the rest of the sentence out before he ran over to me and kicked me in my stomach. I lost my balance and fell directly on the floor.

>Black- (crying) Thomas, why are you doing this to me? I've worked for you for over four years and I've never fucked you over. Do you not have a heart?
>
>Thomas- No, that's one thing I wasn't born with. Sorry. I'll tell you what, though. I want something from you that only you can give me. You know exactly what I'm talking about, too. I want you to dig deep down into the old memory stash and pull out that code of a gold mine. If you choose not to then you choose to become hunted for the rest of your life. (He zipped up his pants.) I think I'm going to love hunting you and everyone around you. (He had an evil smirk.) Give me the codes and I'll let you become a bum in the world. If not, get ready to become prey all around the world. (He walked over, washing his hands, then grabbed a paper towel and dried his hands.) Clean yourself up. (He threw the paper towel at Black.)

He walked out of the bathroom and closed the door behind him. I sat up and tried to think of what he was talking about. What codes was he talking about and why was he so interested to have them? Suddenly I encountered a flashback of when Zane pointed the gun at my father and requested for the code before he shot him, then I came back to reality. I stood up and brushed myself off before I walked out the bathroom. As I left I didn't even bother to look at them because I was completely humiliated. I decide to go home instead of the hospital. I really wasn't in the mood to see my best friend hurt. On my way home I decide to go a different route home. As I turned the corner I spotted Terrance and Samantha arguing while their cars were in the middle of the rode. I became furious and parked the car then got out.

> Terrance- Look, Samantha, I just told you it's over. Can't you get that through your head?
> Samantha- Why? Where did you stay last night? Why won't you tell me?
> Terrance- It's none of your business.
> Samantha- You're my husband; it is my business.
> Terrance- You're my ex-wife-to-be, get it right.

I walked over to them and eyed Terrance hard. He became uncomfortable and signed.

> Samantha- It's her, isn't it? You stayed with this bitch last night, huh?
> Terrance- Yes, I did.
> Black- What's going on? I really want to know who she's calling a bitch.
> Samantha- I like how you stole my husband.
> Black- I like how I stole him, too. I told you I'm a taker.
> Terrance- Okay, look, we're going to be civilized.
> Samantha- Terrance, tell me you don't love me.

He became quiet. I squinted my eyebrows and walked even closer to him.

> Black- You still love her?

He still remained quiet so I smacked him then got back in my Judy's car then left. I began crying instantly.

Samantha- (trying to hug Terrance) So you still do love me, huh?
Terrance- Yes. (He pushed Samantha away.) I still don't want to be
with you, though. (He walked away, getting in his car.)

As I pulled up in front of my house I wiped the tears from my eyes. I was so
hurt and confused that I could kill the next person that dared to deal with me.
I felt so used by Thomas and Terrance that I felt sorry that I ever trusted men.
I got out the car and closed the door. As I walked over to the house I heard a
noise so I reached for my gun. I forgot I tossed it and the other ones were in
the back of my jeep, which was parked by the Leer building.

Black- Shit!

I hurried with the keys trying to get them in the door but they fell. I became
even more nervous as I picked them up and tried again. I just couldn't function
because they fell again and I just knew something terrible was bound to
happen. I picked the keys up again and when I stood back up I was grabbed
from behind. I held my heart as I took a long breath.

Rodney- Are you okay? Did I scare you? I'm sorry, I just was checking
on you. I heard the bad news. I came here last night but no one an-
swered.
Black- I'm fine. Thank you. (She smiled.)
Rodney- (giving Black a hug) How you doing, baby girl?
Black- I'm trying to keep my head up.
Rodney - So, when's the funeral?
Black- Later on this week.
Rodney- (letting Black go) Well, if you don't feel like being bothered
I'll understand. I just wanted to have some dinner with you.
Black- Actually I don't feel like being bothered. Then again I don't
feel like being alone. Hold on.

I opened up the door and put Judy keys back on the table, then headed back out and locked the door. As I turned and looked at Rodney he seemed to be looking for something.

> Black- What are you looking for?
> Rodney- Where's your car?
> Black- Thanks for reminding me. Can you take me to get it?

As I sat in the front seat of my jeep I noticed it wouldn't start up. I knew it wasn't out of gas because I kept a steady tank.

> Rodney- What's wrong?
> Black- My car won't start up.
> Rodney- Does it have gas?
> Black- Plenty, that's why I don't understand.

Rodney put his car in park then got out. He walked over and tapped the hood of my jeep.

> Rodney- Put the hood up.

I did so.

> Rodney- You know why your car won't start up?
> Black- (sitting in the car) Why?
> Rodney- Someone pulled out the distributor cap.

I was hardly shocked at all because I knew exactly who had pulled out the distributor cap. This job was planned, after all. Rodney put the cap back on and I followed him to his house. The dinner as always was fulfilling and I had a marvelous time. Between me being tired, and my back killing me put me directly to sleep. The following morning I woke up and realized Rodney wasn't in the bed so I got up. I looked over at the clock as it read 12:15.

Black- Shit.

I hopped up and ran for my shoes then headed downstairs. Rodney was in the living room reading a newspaper. He looked back once he heard me walk downstairs.

Rodney- Where you going?
Black- I have to go and pick up my daughter and uncle. They're supposed to be arriving at 12:45 P.M.
Rodney- Well, would you mind if I rode with you? I would just love to meet your daughter. Black, I can't hold this back anymore. Even though we don't have a steady relationship I'm falling in love with you.

I began to panic as I froze. I didn't know what to say. I mean the thought was cute and all but I couldn't handle loving two men. I just smiled.

Rodney- I want to be there for your every move you make and be able to support you. Right now you're having a crisis in your life and I know, you know I will be there.
Black- Look, I'm not ready....
Rodney- I know it's too soon but let's take it slow, okay?
Black- Okay.

It was 12:35 as Rodney and I sat two blocks away from the airport. Traffic was completely out of control and it seemed like it would take a while before it would clear up.

Rodney- I wonder what's going on up there.
Black- I don't know but they better hurry up. I don't even know how to explain this to her.
Rodney- Just take your time and do the best you can do.

Meanwhile, while I was stuck in traffic, Thomas, Pink, and Red walked into the airport. They were searching for something. They searched and searched and searched until finally they came upon it. There sat Uncle Sam and Lily in chairs waiting for me to come and pick them up. Red walked over toward them with a camera in her hand.

> Red- Hi, Lily.
> Lily- Hello, Red.
> Red- Would you like to take a picture?
> Lily- Sure, if it's for Mommy.
> Red- Oh, sure, it's for your mommy. In fact, she's the one who sent me to come and pick up you and your uncle.
> Uncle Sam- Well, why wasn't I informed?
> Pink- It was a last-minute arrangement.
> Red- So do you want to take the picture?
> Lily- Come on, Uncle Sam. Say cheese.

Red snapped the picture. It was a Polaroid so it came out immediately.

> Lily- Can I hold the picture? I won't mess it up. I'm a big girl.
> Red- Once you get inside the limo.
> Uncle Sam- Limo. Why, that's so nice of my niece. (He pulled Lily.) Come on, girl, we have a limo to catch.

Red took a marker out of her pocket and wrote "Help me, Mommy" on the back of it. Then she slid it inside of a yellow envelope and placed it on the chair where Lily and Uncle Sam sat. They all headed back outside the airport then pulled off. About five minutes later the traffic began to clear up. Soon we were on the move again. I looked at the clock as it read 12:48 P.M. I already knew they're flight had come in so I just ran inside started looking for them.

Black- Shit, I have to hurry up and find them.
Rodney- Don't worry, she'll be fine; she's with her uncle.

I searched all over the place for them. The cafeteria, bathrooms, and the waiting section, but I still found nothing.

Black- Where could they be?
Rodney- See if the flight is late.

I walked over to a long line and cut everyone that was in the line. People sucked their teeth while others yelled get to the back of the line. I paid not any of them attention. I wasn't worried about them anyway. I was worried about my daughter and uncle.

Black- Excuse me. Did Flight 17 arrive yet?
Worker- You'll have to get to the back of the line, please.
Black- For a question? Look, my daughter is missing and I don't have time to fuck around. Now did Flight 17 arrive or what?
Worker- (snotty) Yes, it did. Now get out of my face.

I balled my fist up and went to punch her but Rodney caught my hand.

Rodney- She's not worth it. Let's find your daughter.

I'm kind of glad I didn't hit that woman or I would have been in jail. Then how or who would get Lily? We searched for three more hours then I decided to go to the police station. Just as I began to walk away in panic I spotted a yellow envelope lying in a chair. A weak feeling ran through my body as I walked over toward it and picked it up. Rodney stood back with his eyes squinted, watching me. I picked up the envelope and stuck my hand inside. I felt something thin but sharp so I pulled it out. I nearly fainted as I looked at a picture of Lily and my uncle. Rodney ran over to me and took the picture from my hand.

Rodney- What's wrong? (He looked at the picture.) Is this them?
Black- Yes. (She was crying.)

Rodney flipped the picture over and read that it said "Dedicated to Mommy."

Rodney- (giving Black a hug) What's going on, girl, you in trouble?

I just couldn't answer him right now so I put my head down and cried. I had a good idea who had them. Thomas was the only person it could be. He wanted some codes I had no idea of and if I didn't give it to him he was going to destruct my whole entire life. I dropped Rodney off home and went to deal with more important things that weighed my back. I went to the police station and they weren't much help. They told me I had to wait another day before they could search. I felt so alone and confused that I went home and drank several cups of scotch. Before I passed out on the couch in the living room I caught a flashback to when my father told me I was always his favorite. The following morning I woke up to some horrible banging on the door. It was so aggravating that it could wake up the neighbors down the road. I was so hungover that I just couldn't get myself to move any faster. The bangs became even louder and annoying that I had no control over swearing.

Black- Hold on, damn it. I said I'm coming.

I walked over and opened the door.

Detective Cargo- Hello, how are you? I just have a couple of questions for you this morning.
Black- You always have questions. Do you ever have any solutions? Did you find my child and uncle?
Detective Cargo- No, we have to wait until tomorrow in the morning to search. Don't worry, we'll find them safe and sound. What I came here for, though, is, um, Samuel Willow is your uncle through your

deceased adoptive mother, Judy Watson, right?

Black- Yes.

Detective Cargo- Okay, I understand that because I did a case on their family a long time ago when their sister Kathy Watson disappeared and no one could find her. Do you know she's still missing? What I don't understand is why there's no record or certificate of you having Lily.

I jumped out of my skin as I sobered up.

Black- That's because I adopted Lily. She's not my real daughter, though I love her like she is.

Detective Cargo- I'm sure you do. In fact, I know you do. Do you mind showing me the adoption agency papers she's from?

Black- Sure, no problem, come inside.

Detective Cargo stepped inside as I ran upstairs and retrieved the information. Thank God I had made arrangements to have a fake adoption agency made for Lily. The only bad thing was once the detective would check the information it would come back phony and I would go down for murder. I walked back downstairs with the information and handed it to the detective.

Black- Is that all?

Detective Cargo- Yes, for now. (He walked out the door.) You must have had a good time last night. Don't worry yourself so much; they'll turn up just fine.

Black- What do you mean?

Detective Cargo- I smell the liquor all over you. (He smiled.) Have a good day.

Black- Detective, how many days will it be until the information comes back?

Detective Cargo- Eight days. Why, is there a problem?

Black- No, I just like to keep up with those papers. They're very important.

Detective Cargo- I'll be talking to you.

Meanwhile, the Long Life Foster Home was filled with hundreds of absent parented children. Derrick Charles was one of them and he also was Blue Charles' son. It was recess time for the children and he loved looking for rocks with funny shapes and colors. He searched and searched and searched until he came upon this huge yellow rock. You could tell that the rock was painted but it sure fooled little Eric. As he bent down to pick up the rock someone stepped on it. Whoever it was wore a black shiny boot with a high heel. As he looked up a woman stood over him.

Pink- What you looking for, kid?
Eric- My name's not Kid.
Pink- Oh, I'm sorry, Eric.
Eric- (confused) How'd you know my name?
Pink- Well, because I was sent to get you. I know your mom and she wants you home, plus I have another cool rock in that limo. You want to come?
Eric- Yeah. (He ran to get in the limo.)
Pink looked around to see if anyone was looking. The coast was clear so she went back inside the limo and closed the door.
Thomas- I see the painting the rock trick worked.

Pink- Like a charm.

Red handed Pink the camera and laughed.

Pink- Would you like to take a picture, Eric?
Eric- Sure. Cheese. (He had a big smile.)

Pink took the picture then stuck it inside a yellow envelope.

Thomas- I want you to get that delivered today. (He looked at Pink.)

I decided to go to the hospital and visit Blue. It was going on a numerous amount of days since I saw her. On my way into the hospital I could hear yelling. It was male voices so I hurried toward Blue's room. As I turned the corner Felix and Isles was arguing.

Felix- You need to mind your business.
Isles- If you put your hands on her again I'll kill you. I promise. By the time my woman gets out of this hospital you better have your shit packed and out.

Felix tried to jump for Isles but two guards came to the rescue and jumped in the way. I was determined to find out why they were arguing.

Black- What's going on? Why are you fighting?
Isles- I can't take it anymore. Go look at Blue's body.

I didn't know what I was looking for but I just went any way. She looked much better as she lied in bed. Her complexion was coming back and she seemed to look stress free. I walked over to her and lifted up her gown. Her body was red with black-and-blue marks for days. Tears formed in my eyes. All I could think about was Grey dying, Judy dying, Lily missing and now this. How could I be so stupid and not realize Felix was beating her? That's why she wore long sleeves when it was 90 degrees outside. My emotions gathered as my fists balled up. All I could feel myself doing was running out the room for Felix. I ran and jumped on him as the two guards moved out my way. We fell to the floor as I still was on top of him. I began punching him as if he were a punching bag. I couldn't stop and God only knew if I wanted to. Tears ran down my face as I continued to pound on him. I could hear him yelling but I didn't care. What about all the times Blue cried and he didn't get off of her? Isles watched with a smile on his face because someone did the justice for him. After a while I could feel some one pulling me off of him. I thought it was Isles but when I looked up it was Rodney.

Rodney- Black, stop it. What are you doing? Isles, why are you letting them fight?

Isles- He deserves it. Besides, I can't do it. I'm on parole and that bitch (looking at Felix) might press charges on me if I get to him.

I stood back and watched Felix get up. He was completely red and embarrassed.

Felix- (out of breath) You crazy bitch. I'll kill you. (He ran toward Black.)

Rodney went to punch Felix but another fist had beaten him to it. I turned around and Terrance stood there vexed. Felix fell to the floor and held his nose as it bled. Rodney eyed Terrance from the side and felt that he was trying to show off.

Terrance- If you ever raise your hand to another woman again I'll cut them off. (He looked at Black.) I need to talk to you.

I looked at Terrance in amazement. I've never seen him so mad and damn, did it look sexy.

Black- Rodney, I'll be right back.

Rodney- You know I think that's pretty rude. He doesn't even care about you.

Terrance- You don't know me worth shit.

Black- Okay, calm down. We don't need any more scenes at the hospital. Rodney, just go ahead and I'll talk to you later.

Rodney- No, you won't. It's over. (He walked away.)

I watched Rodney as he walked away. I knew he was completely mad at me but I already told him I wasn't ready for a relationship. I walked in front of Terrance as the two guards left. We found an area in the hospital where there wasn't a lot of people.

Terrance- So you messing with that lame now?

Black- Aren't you happy with your soon-to-be wife?

Terrance- I don't want her.

Black- No, but you love her. I can't love you if you're loving someone else.

Terrance- Look, I'm sorry that happened, I just got caught up in the moment. You're the only person I want to be with. I just feel like you don't love me because you won't tell me what's going on. How do I know I can trust you? How do I know if your hearts really with me? Tell me something.

Black- Okay, I'll tell you everything after we visit Blue.

Terrance- Black, I….

Black- I swear. Just let me visit her for a little while.

Terrance- (smiling) Okay. Then I want some answers.

Meanwhile, Pink walked in the hospital with some white roses in her hand. She was looking for Blue's room and she didn't have all day to be there. She saw a nurse's station and walked over to it. A nurse was sitting at the desk.

Pink- Excuse me, miss, do you know where Blue Charter's room is?

Nurse- (looking in the computer) One moment. Twelve. It's just right down the hall.

Pink- Thank you.

Pink walked down the hall until she was in front of Blue's room. Once she saw her she smiled then walked in the room.

Pink- Still hanging in there, bitch?

She walked over and placed the roses down on the table then walked closer toward Blue. She stared at her for five seconds then left. Just as soon as she turned the corner to leave Terrance and I turned the other corner toward Blue's room. We walked into her room and spotted the flowers.

Terrance- Oh, I wonder who sent her those pretty roses.
Black- They are beautiful.
Terrance- I think I have an idea who sent them.
Black- Who?
Terrance- Isles.
Black- That can't be, because he's here.
Terrance- That's right. Well, then who sent them?
Black- (walking over to the roses) It's only one way to find out.

I began searching the roses until I came upon an envelope. It was the same kind of envelope that Lily and my uncle's picture were in. I became worried. I stuck my hand in the envelope and pulled out a picture with a little boy on it. I turned it over and it read: "Derrick Charter: dead little boy."

Black- Oh my God. (She held her mouth.)

Just then Isles walked in the room as Terrance walked over and took the picture from my hand and looked at it.

Terrance- Who is this?
Black- That's Eric, Blue's son.
Isles- Son? What are you talking about?
Black- It's a long story.
Terrance- Well, I have all day.

Isles decided to come back with Terrance and me to my place. I knew once I spilled everything Terrance probably wouldn't even look at me as the same. I really didn't want to tell him what was going on but if I didn't it would complicate our relationship.

Black- Well, where should I start? I met Isles, Blue, Grey, Pink, and Red through Thomas. Thomas is a very powerful man and we all work for him. We run errands for him and we're rewarded with pay.

Terrance- What kind of errands?

Black- Robbery errands. Though we have been working for him a long time we've never been to his house, though. We even kill if we have to. I have most of this from my father but most of it's from Thomas also. We're supplied with money, food, and cars. He don't give a fuck about us only his money so that's why we don't play around with his money. He has a bad temper. Normally when we fuck up he'll hurt us in some fucked-up ways. Isles used to run the male group before he went to jail. He's after Thomas because Thomas owes him some money.

Terrance- Do you run the female group?

Black- Yeah. Well, at least I thought I did. I don't know what happened but somehow Thomas got Pink and Red to turn against the group. So that only leaves Blue and me. He already tried to kill Blue and next he's going to kill me. He kidnapped Lily and Eric because I wouldn't give him some codes. I don't know what type of codes he's talking about. Isles, I know you didn't know Blue had a son but this happened a long time ago. Her mother put her son in a foster home and moved away so she didn't know where her son was. I think Thomas also had something to do with Judy's death. Last job when Blue got shot Thomas left us for dead. I had to make a deal with a man named Mr. Owens I just robbed for Thomas in order to get out of that situation. He turned his back on us after all these years. As for today the reason I was fighting Felix was because he was beating her and I didn't know. I don't know why Isles didn't tell me (looking hard at Isles) but I found out any way.

Terrance- So you were the one that put that money on my doorstep.

Black- Yeah, but I told Grey to get you out of the party. Not burn your car down. We had to get you out of the party so we could rob Mr. Mann. I just didn't want you to get hurt. We have bigger things to worry about though because this detective keeps harassing me and I had to give him phony information on Lily today.

Terrance- What do you mean?

Black- That night when I brought Lily home, well, I didn't exactly find her in the garbage. All five of us were outside that night. It was so late and very cold from the rain. We had a lot to drink that night but Red was the worst. She waved down a taxi and robbed the cab driver. Minutes later she shot and killed the driver plus the passengers in the back seat. She stopped shooting once she noticed a baby was in the back seat also. I took the baby and we covered our tracks. Red killed her parents for no reason. That's why we all moved to Manhattan. I had some fake adoption agency papers made but once eight days go by I'm going to jail for murdering three people. I have to find those kids and my uncle then move to New Mexico.

Terrance- What's into Mexico?

Black- Safety. If we don't move to Mexico that detective or Thomas is going to get us. It doesn't matter if he doesn't know you.

Isles- You notice that the men group is still missing, right?

Black- My point exactly.

Terrance- Don't worry. We'll get the kids and Thomas, too.

I fell to sleep while Terrance stayed up all night making phone calls. When I woke up it was the morning so I walked downstairs to look for Terrance. As I got down there he sat up watching a movie.

Black- Good morning, did you get any sleep?

Terrance- No. We have to get ready for a funeral. We're putting her in the ground at twelve this afternoon. All the family's here.

The sweet voice of an angel sang Amazing Grace as tears streamed down my face. The song was so strong that it could attract tears all throughout this world. Terrance squeezed my hand as he tried to cope with it. A tear fell from his eye so I turned and gave him an enormous hug. I could understand his pain because he lost someone so wonderful and no one could take her place. He held me tight and began to sway. I just moved along with him and rubbed his head close to mine. I never realized how much family they had until today. I mean there always were a lot of people at her cookouts but this were if it was a concert. Every one of them was wealthy and well organized in life. Their attitudes said it all. I really appreciated that Isles stayed by our side because Terrance and I really needed it. All I could do was think about Lily. What was she doing? Was she and the others okay? One thing for sure was that Thomas was going to pay. He hurt enough of my good people and I had enough. Another thing I was wondering was, how did he even know that these codes existed? God, there were a lot of things that had to be answered. Being around all this crying just increased my depression. After the burial, Terrance, Isles and I were walking back toward my car to leave, and just when I went to stick the key in the door I felt someone watching me from a distance. I turned toward s the person and looked at them. Whoever it was wore a long gown with a hood on it that covered their entire head. They turned and walked away into the graveyard. Terrance and Isles thought I had lost it and began to wonder who I was looking at and looked in the direction I was looking. They spotted the person and flinched.

Terrance- Who is that?

Isles- You know who that is?

Black- (baffled) No. (She walked to follow the person.)

Terrance- So why are you following them?

Isles- Where you going?

Black- (turning around while she walked) Look, I think I have an idea who it is, just stay there, please. I will only be ten minutes. Trust me on this.

I was a little scared as I followed this person in the graveyard. I began to run a little so that I could catch up but when I did they weren't there. It was as if they just vanished. I started to walk even farther back into the graveyard until Terrance and Isles couldn't see me anymore. I spotted a big tree toward a couple of grave sights and walked toward them. Just as I went to take another step someone spoke from behind me.

Kathy- Don't be alarmed, Black, it's only me, Kathy.

My heart pounded as I turned around.

Kathy- You grew up to look better than what I thought you would. You're beautiful. I'm pretty sure my sister Judy mentioned me to you, or did she forget?

Black- No, she told me about you. She just didn't want me to go looking for you.

Kathy- I know because I wanted to come and find you. Chances are you would not have found me anyway. (She had a weak smile.) Look, I know that there are so many questions that you have to ask me. The question that you want to ask me the most is a question that I don't even know. You do, though, you just have to find it. Twelve years ago your father and I invested in lots of money and property. That was the last thing Zane wanted us to do but we went ahead and did it anyway. We used to do the same kind of work you're doing for Thomas right now.

Black- You know them? Are you working with them because you seem to know so much?

Kathy- Let me finish. Like I was saying. I was in head of my female group and your father was in head of the male group. Somehow Zane found out about our investments and decided he wanted to take it from us. Your father trusted me so much that he told me basically everything. In fact, your mother was going to leave him because she thought he was having an affair with me. Anyway, Zane requested the information on our investments and I gave up mine but nohow was he getting your dad's. In fact, he gave him all the information on his investments except one thing.

Black- The codes.

Kathy- The codes. (She smiled.) Your father knew Zane would kill him and his entire family so he switched his pin number and told no one. Not even me. He said that his favorite little girl would know exactly what he was talking about. The only reason that Zane didn't or better yet couldn't kill you was because you're entitled to the codes once you turn twenty-one years of age. When you were growing up I bet you had that feeling all the time that someone was watching you. Well, you were right. After Zane killed you're family he killed off all the people he had working for him then vanished off this earth and watched you until he could no longer do it. Now he has his son to do the job for him. They're going to hunt you until you give him the codes and I know you don't want to be hiding like me for the rest of your life from him. I think it's good you really have no idea what the codes are right now, but when it's time you better pray you know it. I'll pray for you because these codes depend on your life and when you find the codes I'll give you the key. I'm really going to miss my sister. You know she knew she was going to die because when she first took you in I told her that once you reach over twenty-one he was coming for you. She told me she didn't care and I love and respect her for that. I just wish I had more time to spend with her when she was alive. Terrance turned out to be a great-looking young man. Tell him I said I love him.

Black- I will. Hey, how will I find you to get the key once I find the codes? You don't even live on earth.

Kathy- I'll be around. I can see you. (She walked away.)

I felt relieved but still a little confused. I knew Terrance and Isles would be mad at me because I had them waiting in the car for about half an hour. I watched Kathy disappear in the midst then walked back to the car and got in.

Terrance- Who the hell was that?

Black- That was your Aunt Kathy. She told me basically everything that's going on. A long time ago her and my father worked for Zane. That's the man that killed my family and raped me. That's also Thomas' father. These codes that Thomas wants are the same codes my family was killed for. No one has them, only I do, but the thing is

I don't know them. Whatever this investment is my father gave me must be some shit. She said she's sorry she didn't get the chance to see you grow up and she loves you.

Terrance- My mom always talked about her. I remember her from when I was just a little boy but then she just left. Judy would have killed to see her again. (His attitude was changing.) I'm going to kill that son of a bitch if it's the last thing I do!

Isles- Terrance, calm down, we all going to get our revenge on this mother fucker but we have to figure out how first.

Terrance- Whatever, I need some liquor. Go to the liquor store.

Isles- Don't you have liquor at your house? Why would you want to spend extra money?

Terrance- (angry) I'm not going back to that house!

Isles- I'm sorry, man.

Terrance- (calming down) No, I'm sorry, we just have so much to do. Plus I can't believe my mother gone. Why did this have to happen to me?

Black- Why did this have to happen to all of us? I need a drink anyway.

I walked into the liquor store to get a bottle of Jamaican rum while Terrance and Isles waited in the car. Mr. Mack, the owner, waited behind the counter patiently with a smile.

Mr. Mack- How you doing, Black? Sorry to hear about your Judy, and Lord knows I'm going to miss her. I'll never forget those beautiful eyes.

Black- You liked her, huh?

Mr. Mack- (eyes tearing) I loved her. We used to date back in the days for years. I should have married her, huh?

Black- Yeah.

Mr. Mack- (wiping his eyes) Okay, girl, what will it be?

Black- Jamaican rum. (She dug in her jeans pocket, grabbing a twenty-dollar bill.)

Mr. Mack reached up and grabbed the bottle of Jamaican rum then pulled it down. When I tried to give him the money he pushed my hand away and gave me the bottle.

Mr. Mack- It's on the house.
Black- Thank you. She (gave Mr. Mack a kiss on the cheek.)
Mr. Mack- You even kiss like her.
Black- (laughing) See you later. (She walked out of the liquor store.)

I got back in the car and pulled off. We decided we would go to the beach and relieve some muscles. We stayed at the beach for five hours then went to the hospital to visit Blue. The hospital was so busy that it looked like all the doctors and nurses were running around for fun. As we walked in Blue's room she wasn't in bed so Isles began to panic.

Isles- Where is she? Where is she?
Black- I'm sure she's fine. Maybe they moved her to a different room.

Isles went and looked in the bathroom, when he noticed she wasn't in there he ran to the nurses' station where a nurse sat.

Isles- Excuse me, where's the patient in Room 12?
Nurse- I don't know.
Isles- What do you mean you don't know? Get off your fat ass and find out.
Blue- Isles!

Isles turned around and saw Blue standing there, so he smiled then ran to her. He gave her an enormous hug.

Blue- Ouch.
Isles- (letting Blue go) Oh, I'm sorry, baby. You're walking, that's good.

Blue- (giving Isles a hug) Yeah, it hurts like hell. Thanks for the roses but I prefer red. You've been drinking. I smell it all over your breath. Why... (releasing the hug from Isles) why are you all dressed like you've been to a funeral?

All that Terrance, Isles, and I could do was put our heads down and look at the floor. She hadn't a clue to what we've been through since she been in the hospital.

Blue- What's going on, girl?

Black- Look, I have so much to tell you but now's not the time. I promise I'll tell you everything but I need to know how you feel. Do you feel stable?

Blue- Well, I know one more night in here will do me good. Oh, yeah, that detective was here asking me crazy questions about that night. He said he was told two different sides to what happened. He knows we were in there but he can't prove it because we have an alibi.

Black- Or he might know Mr. Owens is lying. Damn. Look, if you wait until you're discharged to leave then we'll be in a hell of a situation, so tomorrow night me and Terrance is going to come and break you out.

Blue- Damn, you make it sound like I'm in jail.

Black- If we don't come up with a plan fast that's exactly where we'll be, so tomorrow night at 11:30 P.M. Isles, I need you to stay with her just in case.

Isles- Okay.

Terrance and I decided to stay in the house all that night and following day. I went online and found where she lived. Sneaking in the hospital was a tough job but we managed. As we snuck into her room no one was in there but the furniture.

Black- Where the hell are they?

Terrance- I don't know.

I walked over to the bathroom and put my ear to the door but heard nothing. Black- Maybe they're in here.

I turned the knob and opened the door then looked inside. Blue and Isles sat on the toilet making love but as soon as they heard the door open the stopped immediately. I closed the door back then put my hand over my mouth. It was just a mistake. I really didn't know they were in there, plus I told them to be ready at 11:30 P.M. I ran over to Terrance still with my hand over my mouth.

Terrance- What's wrong? What did you see?
Black- (removing her hand from her mouth) They're in there doing it.
Terrance- You mean doing it doing it?
Black- (aroused) Yeah.
Terrance- (grabbing Black close to him) Yummy, that sounds good. (He kissed Black.)
Black- (kissing back) Later.

Blue and Isles came out the bathroom with embarrassed looks on their faces. Pretty soon they began to laugh it off.

Blue- You guys better just mind your business.

Terrance began laughing harder then let me go.

Blue- Where exactly are we going anyway? (She grabbed her white roses.)
Black- We're going to find some answers.

The only place we could go was Thomas' house. I knew it would be dangerous but we were already in danger. On the highway I decided I would tell Blue everything.

Black- Blue.

Blue- Yeah.

Black- You have to be strong for me when I tell you this, okay? Promise me.

Blue- (hesitating) I promise.

Black- Well, where should I start? Judy is dead.

Blue- What? How?

Terrance- Somehow a blow dryer fell into her bathwater. That's why we were dressed like that. Me personally, I think Thomas had something to do with it, though.

Blue- Why would he kill her, though? She has nothing to do with any of this. I'm so sorry, Terrance.

Black- That's not all.

Blue- There's more?

Isles- Yeah, someone has Lily.

Blue - What do you mean someone has Lily?

Black- He means someone kidnapped her from the airport. They also have Terrance's uncle and your son.

Blue- Who, Derrick? That can't be.

Terrance- (reaching into his pocket, grabbing the picture) We're sure. (He gave Blue the picture.)

Blue- (crying) Oh my God. What the hell? Where'd you get this picture, is he alright?

Black- Someone put it in your room in an envelope with those roses. I found that same envelope with Lily and my Uncle Sam's picture in it. Someone's out to get us.

Blue- You mean as in you and I. If you notice no one seems to be bothering Pink or Red. I'm going to get that bitch if it's the last thing I do.

Black- What happened back there?

Blue- After you went back to get her gun off the bed she shot me. It was planned, I could just feel it after you left. You know what she said to me before she shot me?

144

Black- What?

Blue- She said you always thought you were better than me.

Black- Don't worry, we'll come up with something

Isles- So where are we going?

Black- To sneak into Thomas' house.

Blue- What, are you crazy? You're trying to get us killed.

Black- Well, it's better us doing it than him. Besides, who else could be up to this? Blue, he's after me for some codes. The same codes his father killed my family for.

Blue- You mean Thomas is his son?

Black- Yes, and he's planned this from day one. He knew who I was from day one. He's going to kill them and us if we don't stop him.

Terrance- So what did you find out about him?

Black- His name is Thomas Passage and he lives at 491 North Permenter Avenue.

Blue- We don't have a North Permenter in Manhattan.

Black- I know, it's in New Jersey. He travels every day to meet with us. That's why we never been to his house.

Terrance- Do you know if he has any other men around the house?

Black- I don't know but we can find out once we get there.

Blue- You know we have a two-hour ride on our hands. Wake me up when we get there. (She opened up the car window, throwing out the roses.)

It took me a little over two hours to get there due to traffic. When I arrived I noticed I hadn't a clue where to start and the others were sleeping. I decide to keep going until I saw someone. I came to a stoplight then made a right turn. As I drove past the first two houses I saw three little girls playing jump rope outside. I looked at the clock as it read 3:00 A.M. What the hell were they doing outside this type of morning? I parked the car got out then walked over to them.

Black- Hello, what are you doing outside this time of night?

Girl #1- What's it to you, lady?

Girl #2- Yeah, mind your business.

Girl #3- (looking at the other two girls) Cool it. She seems like the only one that cares about us.

Girl #1- What Mama tell you about telling our business?

Girl #2- I'm telling.

Black- Wait, hold up. You three are sisters?

Girl #2- Yeah.

Black- Do you know that blood's thicker than water? In other words you three should stick together no matter what. I wish I still had my two sisters around.

Girl #2- What happened to them?

Black- They were killed.

Girl #3- Oh, how sad. I wouldn't want that to happen to my sisters.

Girl #1- Me neither.

Girl #3- I know you miss them, huh?

Black- Every day. That's why you three should cherish every moment you spend together. Don't ever let anyone hurt you. Besides, it's too late for you girls to be outside. Why don't you go in the house and warm up?

Girl #2- Mama said we can't come in until she's asleep at 4:00 A.M.

Black- What?

Girl #1- Yeah, or we'll get our ass whipped.

Black- Watch your mouth.

Girl #1- Sorry.

Girl #3- Can you help us get out of here?

Black- How, I can't kidnap you.

Girl #2- You don't have to.

Black- So what are you saying?

Girl #3- Can you call the people?

Black- What people?

Girl #1- You know, Child Protective Services.

Black- Are you serious?

Girl #3- As a bad weave.

Black- Okay, but you have to do me a favor also.

Girl #3- What is it?

Black- Tell me where North Permenter Avenue is.

Girl #3- North Permenter Avenue. Oh, you mean Mr. Thomas' place? He owns the whole street. He has a private sign hanging on the gate.

Black- You mean he owns that whole street?

Girl #3- No, I mean he owns that whole property.

Black- You ever see men standing outside his home?

Girl #1- No, but he has four Doberman pinchers inside his gate.

Girl #2- Yeah, lady, watch out for those dogs.

Black- Thank you. (She walked away.)

Girl #3- (running after Black) Hey, we had a deal.

Black- Oh, yeah, I'm sorry.

I could tell these little girls were serious. Besides, after all I did make them a promise. I picked up the phone and called the police. After I was finished I told the little girls to finish playing jump rope; that way the police would see how late it was and they were outside. I went back in the car and started it up. Just then I remembered I forgot to ask them the directions.

Black- Hey, which way?

Girl #3- Just follow the first three lights straight then make a left. Go up the hill but be careful; he has cameras in the front and you'll see it sitting on the hill.

Black- Maybe I'll see you girls around some other time.

Girl #2- Yeah, lady, maybe at the crossroad.

Black- (laughing, pulling off) See you later.

I stopped at a twenty-four-hour store and bought four lighters then drove off and followed the direction the girls told me. As I went up the hill I spotted Thomas' house so I turned off my headlights. I didn't want to alert him of our presence. I couldn't believe what I was seeing. When they told me he had property I had no idea what I was in for. His land stood at least twenty acres. All this time he was handing down chump change to the groups. I became so angry that I had to wake the others.

Black- (lighting up her lighter) Hey, everyone, we're here.

They began waking up from their sleep.

Blue- (waking up, opening her eyes) Why's it completely dark out here? Is this Thomas' property?
Black- Every bit of it. (She handed Blue a lighter.)
Blue- (lighting up her lighter) That son of a bitch was giving us petty cash after going out robbing and killing people every other night. What kind of shit is that?
Isles- (waking up) What are you two complaining about?

I tossed a lighter to Isles then handed one to Terrance.

Terrance- (waking up) What's this for?
Black- Just light it up.

Terrance and Isles lit up their lighters.

Isles- I just know this isn't Thomas' property.
Blue- Well, you're wrong. He's been lying to us from day one. This is why he didn't ever invite us over. To keep the heat from his house and to keep our pockets low on dough.
Isles- Don't feel bad because you're not the one who got the real shitty end of the deal.
Terrance- (looking at Black) You okay?
Black- Yes, I'm fine. (She inhaled deeply.) He has cameras in front of the house. I don't know exactly where they are but be careful.
Isles- He can't see us; it's too dark.

Black- I know but he might have a chance seeing us with these lighters. We can't see without them, plus he has four Doberman pinchers.

Terrance- How did you find out all this?

Black- I just did.

Blue- How are we supposed to get past them?

Black- I have an idea. (She got out of the car, popping the trunk.)

The others got out behind me. I lifted the trunk open then started pulling out guns, giving them away.

Terrance- Where the hell did you get all these guns? Do you have grenades?

Black- Ha, ha. Blue has a nice stash, too.

Blue- Yeah, but I'm not in my hundreds.

Black- Whether you know it, they come in handy. (She put one gun in her side of her pants then held a silencer and wire cutter in her hand while she closed the trunk.)

Terrance- Why do you get two guns?

Black- Well, because they're mine. (She handed Terrance the wire cutter.) You hold the wire cutter. (She walked off, lighting her lighter.)

Terrance- (taking the wire cutter) Damn.

Terrance looked at Isles and found that he was laughing at him. Terrance You think that's funny?

Isles- Very. (He lit up his lighter, walking off.)

I found a path that led to the left side of his house. As I became closer I spotted the cameras. I guess the dogs must have felt our presence because they came to the gate barking. I thought Thomas was going to turn his lights on and come outside but when he didn't I figured he was in a deep sleep or not home.

Terrance- Won't those damn dogs shut up?

Black- They will.

I pointed the silencer and killed each dog. I hated to do it but they would have given us up.

Blue- You know there's a big chance we'll still be seen on those cameras. We have to get them once we get inside.

Black- See, Terrance, you wanted two guns when you was supposed to be already cutting the gate. I don't think so.

Terrance looked at Isles and noticed once again he was laughing.

After Terrance finished cutting the gate enough so that we could get in we crawled underneath, Isles led the way around to the back door. When we got to the back door I discovered it was open.

Black- It's open. Should we just go right in?

Blue- Do you see anyone in there?

Black- No.

Terrance- Well, go inside.

Isles walked in with the rest of us behind him.

Isles- Damn, this house is big. How are we going to find his room?

Black- We're not looking for his room. We're looking for his office. Stick together because we don't know if he's home.

Isles- Let's start from the bottom then work our way up.

After about a half an hour we found his office. No one was home but he had a lock on his door.

Black- Shit! It's locked.

Blue- Well, how are we going to open it? Look under the mat and see if there's a key?

Isles bent down and searched under the mat but found nothing.

Isles- Nope, nothing's there.

We all became quiet for a minute. I then shot the lock off.

Blue- I was waiting to see how long it was going to take you to do that.

Blue pushed the door open then walked in with us behind her. Thomas' office was huge and neater than most so he must have had a maid. A computer sat on his desk along with other office materials. I ran over to it and turned it on. Just as I went to sit in the chair Terrance grabbed my shoulder.

Terrance- Alright, girl, I got this. (He pushed Black lightly from the chair.)

Blue started checking drawers and cabinets as Isles stood by the door watching out.

Black- What exactly are we looking for anyway?
Terrance- A personal diary.

As Terrance entered into the computer it seemed to be giving him some trouble.

Black- What's wrong?
Terrance- (taking a deep breath) I need a password or I can't get in the system. If we get it wrong more than three times it sounds off to the police.
Blue- How many words is it, four letters?
Terrance- No, four numbers. Anyone know any numbers he would use?
Blue- I don't know. Why would he tell us something like that? He barely associated with us. How about you, Isles?
Isles- No.

Black- Well, we could give it two wild guesses.

Terrance- Won't hurt to try.

Blue- How about this group number? One, two, three, four.

Black- Try it.

Terrance- You sure?

Isles- Yeah, go ahead.

Terrance typed in the four numbers then pressed enter. The screen blanked then read: "Please reenter the password."

Blue- Damn, the alarm is going to go off if we don't get it.

Black- Yeah, but we have one more try. Everyone think, think.

Terrance- It's like we came all this way for nothing.

Isles- I got it. How about he replaced numbers instead of letters? Look, there's twenty-six letters in the alphabet. Maybe he numbered his letters.

Terrance- Okay, like W is 23 and the two L's is 12.

Isles- Bingo.

Terrance- Does everyone agree on this?

No one answered back so I guess that meant yes. Terrance typed in the numbers then pressed enter. The screen blanked out then read: "Warning: please reenter the password."

Black- Fuck!

Blue- Oh, God, what are we going to do? We snuck into his house, killed his dogs, roamed through his computer, now we can't get in the program. Just great, I should have stayed in the hospital.

Black- Blue, calm down, we're all in this game together.

Blue- Game? You think this is a game? It's not. Our lives are at stake here.

Black- So are our children. We have to get them back because if anything happened to them I wouldn't be able to forgive myself.

Blue- (waving her hand) Oh, whatever. (She knocked down a photo album from Thomas' desk.) Sorry. (She picked up the photo album.)

As Blue began looking through the photo album her eyes widened.

Blue- Girl, you might want to have a look at this.
Black- Stop going through that damn book.
Blue- Black, just look at it. (She handed the photo album to Black.)

I snatched the photo album from Blue's hand so hard that I knew she could feel the jerk. As I flipped through the pages my stomach fell to the ground as if I were on a roller-coaster. There was a picture of my Zane, Thomas, me, and my father. I was just a little child. Thomas was twelve and I was five.

Isles- What's going on? Someone tell me something.
Black- He planned this whole thing from the start, that son of a bitch.
Isles- Who planned what?

Suddenly I felt like I couldn't breathe. I dropped the book and backed up onto the wall. I closed my eyes as I blanked out. All I could hear over and over again was "Daddy's favorite girl." The room began spinning as I held my head.

Blue- What's wrong with her? Damn it, do something. (She ran for Black.)
Terrance- (grabbing Blue) No, leave her.

The room continued to spin faster as I held my head. A flashback of my sisters picking on me went through my mind. A flashback of my mom and dad arguing went through my mind. A flashback of my family and me at the carnival went through my mind. A flashback of Zane pointing the gun at my mother went through my mind. A flashback of all my father's weapons went through my mind. A flashback of Terrance holding me on the floor when I was younger went through my mind. A flashback of Grey's funeral went through my mind.

A flashback of Lily and Eric went through my mind. A flashback of Uncle Sam went through my mind. A flashback of Judy yelling in the hospital before she died went through my mind. A flashback of Kathy at the funeral went through my mind. I began crying at this point.

> Isles- Terrance, something's wrong with her, man.
> Terrance- No, man, leave her alone. You might hurt her more if you try to help her.

Suddenly a flashback of my father's computer went through my mind. It stopped right in front of my eyes as if they were open. I tried to focus clearly. Suddenly my father appeared at his computer. He seemed to be typing something. By his back being in the way I was unable to tell what he was typing. This flashback was very familiar. In fact, it seemed to be an old memory that just wouldn't leave. Then I appeared in the flashback next to my father. I seemed to be so young and happy at the time. I've never seen a child smile harder than I was. Now I was able to hear the conversation that took place. The only thing was it seemed as if our words were echoing.

Johnny- (echoing) You're Daddy's favorite little girl.

Black- (echoing) I love you, Daddy.

Just then my father grabbed me and held me tight as I giggled.

Johnny- (echoing) What would I do if I didn't have you?

Black- (echoing) Am I really your favorite?

Johnny- (echoing) Yes, honey, always and forever.

I gave my father an enormous hug with my eyes closed. When I opened my eyes I noticed my father had a program on that required a password.

Black- Daddy, what are you working on?

Johnny- A lifetime project.

Black- Can I help?

Johnny- As a matter of fact, you were just the person I was looking for to do the job.

Black- Really?

Johnny- Yeah. Honey, tell me your favorite four numbers.

Black- I have five favorite numbers.

Johnny- Well, only four of them can be used.

Black- Okay, I'll just leave out the last number.

Johnny- Fine. (He smiled.)

Black- Okay, it's 2.

The flashback showed my father typing in the number 2...2.

    The flashback showed my father typing in another 2...7.

    The flashback showed my father typing in a 7...8.

    The flashback showed my father typing in an 8 then he hit enter.

       Black- We probably didn't need the 0 anyway, huh?

       Johnny- Nope, we sure enough didn't. (He smiled, giving Black a hug.)

Just then my flashback vanished from in front of my eyes as I came back to reality. I opened my eyes as tears raced down my face.

       Blue- Girl, you okay?

I just looked at her and continued to cry. I put my head down as Terrance walked over toward me. Then it came to me. Those were the codes that Thomas and his father wanted. I picked my head up and walked past Terrance to the computer.

       Isles- What's she doing?

       Blue- I don't know.

I went up to the computer and clicked on a tiny square box that sat at the top of the screen.

       Terrance- What are you doing?

I paid him no attention. I just continued to do what I was doing. A screen came on the computer that read, enter the codes. I could see Blue and Isles getting close to the door to run once the alarm went off. I typed in 2278 and pressed enter. The screen blanked then read: "Welcome."

Terrance- Oh, shit, you did it. (He smiled.)

Isles- How'd you find his password?

Black- Actually I didn't. Instead I found the codes.

Blue- You mean the codes Thomas and his father was asking for?

Black- Yeah.

Blue- Why the hell didn't you tell us you had the codes the whole time?

Black- Well, I didn't know. A long time ago my father let me make up the password. These are the numbers to my birthdate, I just had to leave out the zero. I just forgot because it was so long ago. When my father used to use this program no one was allowed to go in his room but me. That's why him and my mother used to argue all the time. She thought it was unfair to my sisters.

Terrance- I don't know what you did but you opened up Thomas' diary.

Black- We'll go into that after I find out what are those codes for. Go ahead, Terrance. Isles and Blue, you two are straight scaredy-cats.

Isles- You remember what happened to me before? I'm just trying to get a head start. (He smiled.)

Black- (laughing) Yeah, okay.

Terrance managed to get into the program and pulled up some interesting information. He pulled up a map and address of some storage place in Philadelphia.

Terrance- You might want write down this information, plus I can also get a printout on this map. I want to know, why would he keep this map on his computer?

Black- (grabbing a pen and piece of paper off Thomas' desk) Well, that's because he or his father never been able to get into this program without these codes. He doesn't even know I've activated this program. (She copied the information off the computer.)

Terrance- Good, and he doesn't have to know. We're taking this disk with us after we copy that map. You finish copying that down?

Black- Yeah.

Terrance- Good, now we're going into his diary. (He went into Thomas' diary, reading to himself.) Hey, listen to this. "Today she came to me with that gorgeous twinkle in her eye and told me some astounding news. In a way I loved it but then again I couldn't cope with it. Why now, it was just a stupid mistake. I'm not ready to be a father. I put an end to the first one and I'll do it again."

Blue- What the hell does that mean?

Black- (shocked) It means he was the father of Grey's baby.

Isles- Well, I'll be damned.

Terrance- Grey was pregnant?

Black- Yeah, by Thomas, that's why she kept it as a secret.

Blue- (feeling sick) Well, I would, too.

Isles- (smirking) Stop it, that's your friend.

Blue- I know but I thought she would have better taste in men.

Black- You guys, don't you see? Thomas really loved Grey and he wanted that child. He just couldn't because by him trying to collect my inheritance then get rid of me if anything ever happened to him her child would get that inheritance, and that would put her back in the picture. Believe me, he's sorry he had to kill her.

Isles- He'll be even sorrier once I get my hands on him.

Blue- That slimy bastard.

Terrance moved the arrow down with the mouse and came upon some different information with a different date.

Terrance- He wrote that on the job you did with Mr. Mann he was missing $10,000. He wrote it was supposed to be $80,000 and he only received $70,000.

Just then I had a flashback of when Mr. Mann directed me to $80,000 and Red counted out $70,000.

Black- Red was stealing from Thomas. That's probably how he got her to turn against me by making her a proposition.
Terrance- Yeah, well, he must have made Pink one too, it just doesn't say why. Instead it says Pink, you sneaky lady.
Black- I don't know. What else?

Terrance moved the arrow down farther and came upon some information on a hotel.

Terrance- The Anacar Hotel in New Hampshire. You think that's where he's hiding them?
Black- I don't know but we'll find out. Is there anything else?
Terrance- No. Wait, he wrote "termination of men 491 Wimberley Road in Los Angeles."
Blue- Once again, what does that mean?
Black- Hard to say.
Terrance- The last thing he wrote is "hit woman 64 Parasite Avenue, Virginia."
Isles- What's he doing with a hit woman? I don't know what he plans to…

Isles couldn't even finish the sentence because what Thomas wanted her for.

Terrance- So what are we going to do?
Black- Listen, first thing is we have four places to check. Right now we only can make it to two because we don't have enough time. We also have to catch up with Mr. Owens before he thinks I'm pulling his chain.

Blue- So which two will we have to skip?

Black- Philadelphia and the hotel.

Blue- No, we can't. Our children might be in there.

Black- I know but we really have to find out who's this hit person is and who's she for? Plus he terminated something Blue and he's not the Terminator.

Blue- (walking away angry) He's going to kill....

Black- No, he's not, but if we're going to get them back we have to know what we're getting into.

Blue- Alright, let's just hurry up so we can get to that hotel.

Black- You and Isles is going to have to check out the hit person while Terrance and I see what he terminated. It might not be good. I'm going to give you extra vest and guns just in case before I drop you off at your house, Blue, before you go to Los Angeles.

Blue- I've always wanted to go there.

Black- Don't go there and gamble, girl, we have things to do.

Suddenly we heard a television turn on. I became faint with panic as Terrance flagged Isles to go to the window to see if Thomas was here.

Isles went to the window and peeked out but noticed no one was out there.

Isles- No one's out there.

We became a little puzzled.

Terrance- (whispering) Follow me, we have to get out of here. (He got out of the chair.)

Black- (whispering) No, we have to see who's in the house and get those tapes. You forget we're on camera. Once he sees that we were here he's coming to kill us. Now get the disk and come on.

Terrance- (sucking his teeth but going back to the computer) Damn, girl. (He closed the program on the computer then took out the disk.)

After I saw Terrance take the disk out I put my gun up and walked in the direction of the television. Blue followed right behind me. Isles waited in the room for Terrance while he put the disk in his pocket. Terrance looked at Isles and found that he was smirking.

> Terrance- Let me guess, you're laughing at me? (He walked out to follow the girls.)
> Isles- Yeah. (He followed Terrance.)

Meanwhile, Lily, Derrick, and Uncle Sam were tied up and put in a closet without a pinch of light. Often Uncle Sam had to calm the children down due to the dark and being scared. The sound of the closet opening scared them all. Thomas stood there and looked at them. He carried a black plastic bag, which he threw over to Uncle Sam.

> Thomas- Here, eat what you can, while you can.
> Uncle Sam- How am I supposed to eat? What are you going to feed me?

Thomas pulled out a knife and headed toward Uncle Sam with a look on his face that meant he wanted to kill. He bent down in front of Uncle Sam then rubbed the knife down his face. Uncle Sam became angry because he felt helpless. Thomas cut the rope from his hands and looked at him.

> Uncle Sam- What about the children? Untie them so they can eat.

Thomas leaned over and did so.

> Thomas- If you try anything I'll kill you, old man.
> Uncle Sam- I don't give a fuck about you.

Meanwhile, I insisted on knowing who was in that room with the television. I put my ear up to the door then listened. I could hear someone clicking the remote and some type of machine on. I pointed to the door so everyone would know that was the door we were going in. I started with three fingers and counted down to one before I turned the knob and went in. As I walked in the room I saw an old man lying in bed hooked up to a breathing machine. As I became closer the man looked more and more familiar. There was the moment I waited for ten years. I began crying as if someone was constantly stabbing me. Here lay the man who murdered my family then raped me. He had fallen asleep on the remote. I understood that God was going to deal with him but I got to him first. All I could think about and wanted was revenge.

Terrance- Is this the man who did that to your family?
Black- Yes, and he's going to pay.

I walked over to the other side of him and grabbed two latex gloves from the box that held them and put them on. I then began roaming through his drawers looking for something. Tears fell down my face as I looked. Then I found it. I pulled the scissors out and closed the drawer back. I thought some-one was going to stop me but instead they just watched as if they wanted me to do it. I hesitated then cut his breathing tube.

Black- (looking at Zane) This is all your fault.

I continued to watch him gasp for air until he lay still with his eyes closed. I felt ashamed but relieved. I know my father would have wanted me to kill him anyway. I whipped the last tears that fell from my eye then turned and looked at the others.

Black- We have to get those tapes, wipe down the place then get the hell out of here. Hurry.
Isles- Terrance, give me the disk so I can make a copy of that infor-mation and map. It'll come in handy.

After we retrieved the tapes we cleaned every area that we touched and got the hell up out of there. On our way back before we got to the highway I went through to check on the little girls. As I drove past two police cars and a social worker's car was parked in front of their house. The little girls were being put into the social worker's car while two different policemen escorted their parents in two different police cars.

Blue- Wow, I wonder what happened there.

Terrance- Those poor kids, how sad.

Black- Yeah, well, at least they're in better hands.

I stopped at my house and got Blue and Isles extra guns and vests before I dropped them off at her house. We didn't realize Felix's car in the driveway because the garage door was shut.

Terrance- You guys, hurry up and get on the move. We'll meet you at nine o'clock on 81st Street. Don't leave one another alone for a minute. See you later. (Black pulled off in the car.)

I pulled off and headed for Los Angeles.

Isles- Blue, you have your keys on you?

Blue- Yeah, but I have to use the bathroom first.

Isles- Hurry and give me the keys so I can start the car.

Blue- (tossing the keys to Isles) Here, I'll be right back.

As she ran to her front door she noticed it was open so she pushed it in. She looked inside but found nothing. Suddenly her insides felt as if they were about to explode so she ran to the bathroom and closed the door. When she was finished she washed her hands then turned off the light and headed for downstairs until she heard some noise. It sounded as if it were voices coming from her bedroom. She turned around and headed for her bedroom, but when she heard a female laugh she stopped right where she was. Once the laughing stopped she continued to walk. That laugh sounded so familiar so she stuck her head into the bedroom and peeked in. There was Pink and Felix having sex in her bed. Immediately her heart fell into a million pieces. It wasn't the fact that he was cheating; it was who he was cheating with. She wanted to jump on the both of them but instead she just slid the door back up. Isles sat waiting in the passenger side of her car when he saw her walk out with a knife and bat in her hand. At first he thought she was just bringing them until he saw her break the front windshield of Felix's car. Then she began stabbing his car. Isles jumped out of her car and ran for her. Once he got to her he took the bat and knife from her then put it in the back of her car and closed the door. Blue continued to kick and pound on his car with just her bare hands.

> Isles- (grabbing Blue) What's wrong with you? Stop it, stop it! (He shook Blue.) Stop!
> Blue just put her head down on Isles' shoulder and began crying.

Meanwhile, Thomas' limo pulled up to a stop at his house and he got out before the driver could get out and open his door.

> Thomas- (looking at his driver) You're too slow, you're getting old.

Thomas walked up six steps before he noticed that his dogs hadn't barked or jumped on him yet. He walked back down the stairs and whistled for his dogs. When he noticed they didn't come he walked back down the steps and walked toward the backyard. As he approached the back of his house he saw his four dogs lying in blood so he ran for them.

> Thomas- What the fuck? Who....

Thomas became emotional and put his head down. He saw that his gate had been cut and he immediately thought of his father. Just then he came to the conclusion that someone robbed him. He pulled his gun from the back of his pants and ran for the back door. It was open so he walked inside. He inhaled deeply then he searched his house for ten minutes until he came upon his office. His lock had been shot completely off so he kicked the door open and looked inside. No one was inside so he hurried to his father's room and opened the door. His father was in bed so he was relieved. He closed the door and took a couple of steps before he noticed he hadn't heard his father's breathing machine and turned back around. He opened the door and ran for his father then grabbed his hand. There he lay stiff as a board. Thomas' pride kept him from crying so he just put his head down and held his hand.

Terrance and I had just arrived to Los Angeles. It was quite a trip but we made it. When we arrived to the address Thomas wrote down in his computer we became very confused. The building seemed to be condemned and very old.

> Black- Is this the right address?
> Terrance- Yeah.
> Black- This building looks too creepy.
> Terrance- I know. I'm afraid to go inside.

I got the impression that by us going into this creepy building we were going to come out with some bad news. We got out the car and walked inside of the building. The only light we had were those lighters I bought from the store so we lit them up. I was scared but I didn't want Terrance to know that. We saw some stairs and went up them. Once we reached the top an odor so strong hit our noses that we nearly vomited.

> Black- God, what's that awful smell?
> Terrance- (covering his nose) It smells as if something died.
> Black- Please don't speak the truth.

As we proceeded to walk toward a closet the smell became worse. I knew the smell was coming from inside the closet. Meanwhile, Blue was still upset. In fact, she was so upset that she hadn't said a word since they left the house.

> Isles- Look, I'm sorry you had to see that. I told that clown I wanted
> him out of your house by the time you came home anyway. I know
> it's got to be one of the worst things to see but one thing I can assure

you is I'll never disrespect you like that. I promise. When you learn to love me....

Blue- Learn? Isles, you know I love you so don't act like that. It's just that I know she's been the one calling my house and I know Thomas caught them together, that's why he called her a naughty girl. They have my son and he doesn't even know me. If I get him back where would we go because I'm going straight to jail once that detective gets a hold of me. I wish I never gotten into this gang shit. Being a bum is safer.

Isles- Now you're talking crazy. Being a bum is not safer and when you were a bum you still were not a bum. Yeah, your clothes were tacky the first day we saw you but when you got all fixed up I knew I had to have you. I love your son, though you never told me about him. One thing that you have to promise me is that you won't keep any more secrets from me. You got it?

Blue- You have my word.

Isles- (grabbing Blue's hand) Don't worry, we'll figure something out, but in the meantime we have to walk up the block and around the corner. Parasite Avenue is just ahead. (He took off his seatbelt then let go of Blue's hand.)

Blue- We're here already?

Isles- Yeah. (He opened up the car door.)

They stepped out the car and started walking until they came to the corner then turned. Once they got around the corner Isles saw a tree directly across from 64 Parasite Avenue.

Isles- Let's go in those bushes by that big tree. 64's just across the street.

Thomas watched as the coroner put his father's body in the back of the van. His world felt as if it were tearing away slowly but surely. He thought the day would never come to see his father die. He always thought he would go before his father. All of this stress had him thinking. He walked inside his house then closed the door. He didn't want to see the coroner pull off with his father in the back. He had switched his father's breathing tube so they would think his old age just caught up with him. Thomas walked back to his office and closed his door as if there were no bullet holes in his door. He sat down and stared at the door. Why did today have to be the day his father died? Just then he looked at his computer and noticed the screen was still on. He sat up and became alert. He then began looking on the floor to see if he saw shoe prints but instead he found his photo album. He turned his computer on and went into his diary. Thomas began laughing.

Thomas- Well, I see she found the codes. Good girl, and I see you made several copies and you took the disk.

He began laughing even louder. He laughed as if someone was tickling him. Last night before he left he had put a new set of printing paper in his printer. Who would want to go through his computer though, of all the goods he had in his house. He knew exactly who had been in his house, me. He picked up the phone and dialed Red's number.

Red- Hello?
Thomas- You know who this is. Meet me at the bowling alley right now. Make sure you call Pink.
Red- Okay. (He hung up the phone.)

My heart pounded as we stood by the closet door. I could hear Terrance's heart pounding through his shirt.

Terrance- Open it.
Black- You open it.
Terrance- Why?
Black- Well, because you're a man.
Terrance- (straightening up) Oh, yeah.

He hesitated a good two seconds then opened the door. I was expecting to find a couple of bodies but instead nothing was inside. The weird thing was the smell became worse.

Black- If there's nothing in there then what's that smell?
Terrance- I don't know. (He backed up.)

Terrance took three steps backward. By the fourth step he stepped on a board, which lifted up in the closet. I looked at him as he looked at me. He walked back over toward the closet then lifted up the board. After he was done he did another then another then another. Once he looked in he covered his face and walked back toward me. Taking a chance I walked over toward the missing boards and looked in. There I saw all four of the male group men dead. They had been tied up and shot in the head. I took a deep breath and backed up onto the wall as I blanked out. I began to panic because if he had no sympathy for them he most certainly didn't have any for us. Suddenly I could feel someone shaking me.

Black- What, what?
Terrance- Why do you keep on doing that? I really hate it when you do that. You scared the hell out of me. What do you know those men?

I was so betrayed and hurt. I was worth more than the average woman and Thomas wanted to kill me.

Black- (crying) I can't believe he killed them as if they were no one.
Terrance- Who?
Black- The group. He killed Boogie, Mitch, Cash, and Leon. This was the male group that Isles was training before he went to jail. Thomas told us that they were on vacation and would be at the Jumble. That's where several big bosses come together and eat, gamble, and trade men. Thomas loves to gamble his whole entire income away. He's never lost.

Terrance- Never?

Black- Never.

Terrance- I don't really know this Thomas character but I don't like him much. When's the Jumble?

Black- It's in four days. If we don't find them then….

Terrance- Don't think like that. We'll find them, I promise. Now let's get out of here.

Meanwhile, Isles and Blue sat waiting to see something or someone move. The lights were off in the house and the car was missing from the driveway. Blue felt aggravated but this wasn't the place or time. She didn't know which was worse, being shot or catching her husband in bed with an enemy.

Isles- You okay?

Blue- Yeah, I've had worse days.

Isles- Like?

Blue- Like, when you didn't make it out that building.

Isles- I went to jail.

Blue- I know. Like the first day Felix hit me and acted as if nothing ever happened? Also when you walked in on me in that bathroom and saw my battered body.

Isles- I was hurt. I wanted to kill that man that night.

Blue- So did I.

They stared at each other and felt a moment of love and relief. Isles leaned over and gave her a kiss so wonderful that it made her insides tingle as her body shivered. She left all her dilemmas to the side and relaxed. After ten seconds they departed. He kissed her on her forehead then stroked her hair. She smiled as she looked into his gorgeous eyes. Suddenly they heard a front door open so they hurried to the spot where they could peek out of and looked out of it. Some lady next door to 64 Parasite stepped outside and watered her garden. She hummed a tune we were not familiar with as a car pulled up to the driveway of 64 Parasite then came to a stop and turned their lights off. The back door opened and two little girls and a boy ran from out the back seats and into the backyard. They were in such a rush that they didn't even close the door back. The driver side of the car opened and Samantha stepped out. Isles and Blue were shocked as they looked at her to make sure that was Samantha. It was and she was the hit woman.

Blue- (whispering) What the fuck is going on?

Isles- (whispering) I don't know.

Neighbor- Hi, Vanessa, how you doing?

Samantha- Fine, and you?

Neighbor- Good, real good. Where's your husband?

Samantha- Chris, he's working.

Neighbor- Well, tell him my husband asked about him. I'm having a birthday party for Sean. Let the kids come over.

Samantha- Okay, I will. (She walked in the house, closing the door.)

Isles and Blue looked at each other.

Blue- Her real name is Vanessa and she's already married with children. Right now we have to hurry back to Manhattan and we have to hurry. They're not going to believe this.

Pink and Felix were leaving from Blue's house and just stepped in to the driveway. Felix hadn't noticed his car because he was looking at Pink. Once he noticed how wide her eyes were he turned around and looked. His jaw fell to the cement as he looked at his car.

Felix- What the fuck?

Pink- Damn, I'll have to take a cab. I should have brought my car.

Felix- Did you do this?

Pink- How could I do this if I was riding you?

Felix- Don't lie to me, bitch.

Pink- I'm not lying.

Felix began to panic as he paced the floor. He started looking around as if he were crazy then he realized Blue's car missing.

> Felix- Where's the car? Where's the fucking car? She did this to my car.
> Pink- Well, maybe she saw me and you fucking and she fucked up your car.
> Felix- I'm going to kill that crazy, shot-up bitch.

Pink's cell phone began to ring. Once she recognized the number she answered it.

> Thomas- If I have to tell you one more time to get over here at the bowling alley you'll have toenails for teeth.
> Pink- Okay, I'm on my way. I have to take a cab. (She hung up the phone.)

Detective Cargo was sitting at his desk reading the report on Thomas' father, Zane Passage, when he came to an idea. He put the report down, got up, and opened the door to his office. He was going to look for Darlene because she was the best at getting information from computers. Finally he found her sitting at her desk.

> Detective Cargo- Darlene, listen, I need your help.
> Darlene- Look, I have exactly one hundred favors to do for other people. Everyone has been nagging me, Darlene do this, Darlene do that. What make you so damn special?
> Detective Cargo- (throwing two hundred dollars on her desk) Here's two hundred for you.
> Darlene- (picking up her pen and pad) Okay, what do you need?
> Detective Cargo- I need the following reports. The case on the Burks family in Texas, the report on the murder of the Cummings family in Texas, the report on Judy Watson's murder at her home here in Manhattan, the report on the robbery at Mr. Mann's nightclub, the report on Black Cummings' missing daughter, the report on the missing

child of Derrick from the foster home in Durham.

Darlene- I see why you gave me this money. I also see you're on to something.

Detective Cargo- That's our secret. (He smiled and walked away.)

Thomas was frustrated because this hadn't been such a good day for him. Pink and Red were the ones he would take it out on. It turned out he was hiding the kids at the hotel and he had to hurry to the hotel before we made it there. Thomas, Red, and Pink pulled up to the hotel.

Thomas- You two better pray those people are still in that room. If they are get them in this car and hurry.

Red and Pink stepped out the limo and walked to the door. Red stuck the key in the door and opened it. Pink walked in and went straight toward the closet with Red behind her then opened it. Uncle Sam and the children were still in there sleeping so Red walked over to him and smacked him so hard he woke up. Pink laughed as she picked Derrick up.

Red- Let's go, you old fool.

Uncle Sam- Girl, wait until I get these cuffs off, muff diver.

Pink began laughing louder as he stood up and walked out the door and into the limo with Red and Pink behind him. Lily opened her eyes as she pretended to be asleep. She took out her hair bow and threw it in the corner then closed her eyes back. Red came back in and picked her up then walked out the door and closed it.

Terrance and I sat impatiently waiting for Isles and Blue to return. I wondered what was taking them so long.

Terrance- You think they made it back okay?

Black- They had to.

We waited for another ten minutes then they pulled up and parked.

Terrance- They're here.

As they got out the car and shut the door I became jittery in my stomach. Their faces were pale as if they had just seen a ghost.

Black- What's wrong?
Blue- You first.
Black- Okay. We went to the address and the funny thing was it was a condemned building.
Isles- Really?
Terrance- Yeah, so we got inside and a smell and you couldn't even bear with a paper bag hit us in the face soon we hit the building. As we go upstairs the smell get worse and it's coming from a closet so we opened it.
Blue- What did you find?
Black- The men group. They were all killed and buried underneath the closet.
Isles- You talking about the men group I trained?
Black- Yeah.
Isles- That's fucked up.
Black- I know.
Terrance- So what did you guys find?
Blue- Are you ready for this? Well, we went and checked out the address. We waited for a while then Samantha pulls up.
Terrance- (confused) What Samantha?
Isles- Your almost-wife was Samantha. The only thing is her name isn't Samantha, it's Vanessa. She's already married with kids and a husband.
Black- Are you sure?
Blue- We're positive.

I looked at Terrance as he contained a hurtful look on his face. He didn't want to show it because we were around but it stuck him deep in his heart.

Isles- I don't think she was hired to kill you, man; she was hired to kill Black.

Black- Me, huh? Well, if we wouldn't have paid Thomas a visit she probably would have succeeded.

Terrance- What does her husband look like?

Blue- We don't know, he wasn't around. Sorry it happened like that.

Isles- You know, we should check the hotel room while we can. God knows what he'll do next.

Terrance and I jumped in my car while Blue and Isles jumped in hers. We pulled off and headed for the hotel. Soon the time had come. We arrived at the hotel.

Blue- What number are we looking for?

Isles- 4a.

The number we were was at was 8c so I drove down until I was close to 5c and parked the car.

Terrance- Everyone, take your guns out. Get in and get those kids and my uncle. If they're not in there get the hell out.

We got out the car and headed for 4a. Terrance, Blue, and I stood back as Isles kicked the door in. Terrance ran in first then we followed. I had my gun up and I was hungry to pull the trigger. Terrance opened up the bathroom door but no one was inside. We became disappointed. I noticed the closet Blue was standing next and flagged for her to move.

Black- Watch out, Blue. (She pointed her gun at the closet.)

Blue opened the door and jumped back. Once again no one was inside but I thought I saw something in the corner of the closet. I bent down and looked closer to find that it was Lily's hair bow. I picked it up and showed the others.

Terrance- What is it?

Black- It's Lily's hair bow. She threw it in the corner to let me know that she was here. God, I hope she's okay.

Blue- Oh, so all you care about is your daughter? What about Eric and your uncle?

Black- Look, you know what I meant. I care about all of them.

Blue- No, you don't you only care about you and yours.

Black- What you flipping out on me for? I'm not the one that took your kid or shot you.

Blue- I know it was Pink. She took them, shot me, now she's fucking my husband. She's even been the one calling my house.

Black- What are you talking about?

Blue- Look, it doesn't even matter, just leave me alone.

Black- So what are you saying?

Blue- I don't fucking want to be bothered!

Black- Fine, then get the fuck out. I'll find the children and my uncle on my own then I'll take him in with me.

Blue- Why, he doesn't know you and you don't know him.

Black- Neither do you.

I must have really hurt Blue's feelings because I could see a tear form in her eye. Then she turned around and left with Isles right behind her. I didn't mean to say that; it just slipped out. I looked at Terrance and the look he gave me told me he was also mad. Maybe I was wrong for saying that but she started it.

Terrance- You're wrong and you know it. Drop me off at a hotel until you get your shit together. (He walked away.) I'll be in the car waiting.

I didn't understand why everyone was so mad at me. I know I was always trying to be on top and in charge. I walked out the room and got in the car then started it up. I pulled off and headed toward a hotel for Terrance. He hadn't said a word to me since we left. I pulled up to the hotel and stopped. Terrance opened the door and got out but didn't close the door back. He just walked off. I leaned over and closed the door back then pulled off. He waited until he couldn't see my car then walked across the street and checked into another hotel. I stopped at a gas station and brought a pregnancy test then went home and took a nice, long, hot shower. After I got out the shower I decided I would take the pregnancy test so I did. I was so tired that I fell asleep before I could read the results. The following morning I woke up on the couch with the pregnancy test in my hand. I wiped my eyes then headed upstairs to get the box off the sink. I looked at the test and it had two lines going across it. I looked at the box to see what it meant. I couldn't believe what I was seeing. The test indicated that I was pregnant. Oh my God, I was going to be a mommy. Suddenly I felt depressed. I wasn't a good mommy because my first child was kidnapped and I was even putting this child's life in danger. How was Terrance going to feel about this anyway? I placed the test inside the box and threw it in the garbage in the bathroom. I went back downstairs and began to wonder what I was going to do. Then it hit me. I jumped up and put some clothes on and hopped in my car and headed for the cemetery, which Judy was buried in and began looking around.

Black- Kathy! Kathy! I need your support, Kathy.

I felt ridiculous calling this woman in a graveyard. I doubted if she was even there but how else was I supposed to find her once I found the codes? I waited for another six minutes then headed back toward my car.

Kathy- Sorry I'm late. I see you came to your senses and found the code.
Black- Yes, I did. Now where's this key you told me you had for me?
Kathy- (reaching in her pocket, giving Black a funny-shaped key)

Here you are.

Black- (taking the key) This key is shaped funny. (She looked at the key.)

Kathy- Well, I really don't think you have much time to do things. You should be on your way.

Black- Kathy, would you come with me? I know you would like to see this project my father has hidden for so many years.

Kathy- That would be lovely, but I can't stay long, okay?

Black- No problem.

Kathy and I had quite a travel. When we arrived it seemed that we were in the complete woods.

Black- Are we even in the right place?

Kathy- I believe so. Whatever your father has I'm pretty sure he wasn't going to just leave it in the open.

Black- What do you mean?

Kathy- Come on, let's just look around.

Kathy and I continued to walk around until we came upon a large area filled with grass. It was so huge you could fit a carnival there.

Black- I really don't know what we are looking for but I know we're not going to find it any time soon. (She walked into the center of the grassy area.)

Kathy- Well, we haven't even started looking yet.

Black- I know but there aren't even any numbers around here. How are we going to find it?

Just then I fell into the ground. I screamed until I hit the bottom then I jumped up real quick. As I looked back up to where I fell Kathy stood there with a tremendously big smile on her face. I couldn't help but to laugh. Once I looked back down to where I was I seemed completely confused.

Kathy- What is it? Help me down there.

After I helped Kathy down into where I fell we began looking around. She began feeling on the walls to see if she could find a light switch. Finally she found it and turned it on. Once she turned on the lights I couldn't believe what I was seeing. My father had a computer and several devices on a switchboard. I ran over and turned on the computer. Once I did that the switchboard began to light up.

Black- Damn. (She smiled.)
Kathy- I see why he kept this as a secret. All of this stuff is worth a fortune. See what some of those buttons are for.

I sat down at the computer and began messing with the program. I stuck in the key and entered the code and it caused all of the walls to flip inside out. Once all of the walls were flipped inside out thousands of different types of guns were attached to them. They ranged from the year 1819 to 2003.

Black- Damn, Dad.

I began to mess around with the computer again and this time when the walls flipped it was grenades, bulletproof jackets, and maps of all the states in the world. My smile became bigger because my father wasn't just an ordinary man. He really worked for what he wanted. I fiddled with the computer again and watched the walls flip. It was a large map to Mexico. The map was so big that all four walls held it.

Kathy- Do you understand now, Black?
Black- I sure enough do. He knew I would need this because he knew Thomas was coming for me. He planned out this whole thing for me. He even knew I would then flee to Mexico. He was helping me this whole time, though he's gone.

Kathy- Exactly. See, I don't know if you know what you have here in your face but I'll explain it to you. This is what your father worked so hard to get to you so you must take care of it. If the government ever got they hands on this what do you think they would do?
Black- Throw my ass in jail and ban this from America.
Kathy- Right and wrong.
Black- What do you mean?
Kathy- I mean right they would throw your ass in jail because this is enough ammo to serve you a lifetime sentence. Even Lily's great-grandchildren couldn't finish a bid like this for you; their great-grand-children would have to finish it up. I mean wrong because if the government ever found this they wouldn't ban it from America. They would keep it for themselves. There's no one stupid enough to throw away a lifetime of ammo.

I thought about what Kathy said for a while because she was right. I put my head down and spotted a green button.

Black- I wonder what that button's for.
Kathy- Push it.

I pushed the button then waited for a reaction. It took a while but then a little compartment in the wall pushed out. I walked over to it and looked inside. There was a duffle bag stuffed inside. I opened the bag and nearly fell backwards.

Kathy- What is it?

I stuck my hand into the bag and pulled out some money.

Black- I'm loaded.

I stuck the money back in the bag and felt around the bag. I felt something hard and sharp so I picked it up. It was wrapped up and read to Kathy. I handed her the object wrapped up and watched as she unwrapped it. When she was finished she held a glass box with two guns in it.

Kathy- (crying) Oh my God.
Black- What is it?
Kathy- It's the first guns your father and I ever used on a job. One day it just popped up missing and when I asked your father he said he didn't see it. He tricked me. (She looked at Black.) I love that man. I want you to take good care of this place and if you ever need guidance this is where you come to. This is your father.

After I gave Kathy a little bit of money I stayed a while and learned some things about that place. When I became tired I decided to go home and cook. Meanwhile, Terrance sat in a bush waiting for the clock to strike nine. He had two minutes to go. He sat impatiently with his gun in his hand. He was going to find out if what Blue and Isles told him was true. True about her life, children, and marriage. Finally it was time so he stood up and looked to see if anyone was outside. When he noticed there wasn't he jotted out the bushes and ran across the street. He ducked down behind Samantha's car and looked at her windows. Once he saw the last light cut off in the house he ran around to her back door and turned the knob. It was locked so he took his wallet from his coat pocket and took a credit card out. He picked the lock until it opened then put the card back in his wallet and into his coat pocket. He pushed the door in and went inside. No one was present so he began walking through the house. He walked lightly and careful so he didn't wake any of the children. The hallway was pretty long and it took forever to get to the end of it. Once he did two doors sat in the back. One of the doors had a "do not enter" sign on them so he turned the knob with the do not enter sign on it and walked inside. He pushed the door back up but he didn't close it. Inside was beautiful as if it were an office. He began looking inside of the drawers. He wanted to see what the children looked like so he began going through the pictures that were in the drawers. The children were so beautiful but their mother was up to no good. He continued to go through the rest of the pictures. When he got down to the last picture Samantha stood there with a smile. The funny thing was she cut whoever else that was in the picture out. Terrance wiped the pictures off and put them back then opened another drawer. He began searching underneath the papers that were in the drawer. He felt something so he pulled it out. It was the key that he had made for his mother. Suddenly he had a flashback to when they were having dinner and he gave the key to his mother. He became furious and put the key in his pocket, as he continued to go through the drawers. He continued to feel around in the drawer. Suddenly he felt some type of leather, so he pulled it out. It was a wallet so he opened it up and began going through it. He looked through it finding nothing but insurance and credit cards. He spotted something tucked on the side of the wallet so he took it out. It was a New York State identification card. As he looked at it his eyes widened. Just as he turned around he was hit on the back of the head with a lantern. He fell to floor knocked out. It was only 8:30 P.M. when my doorbell rang. I was hoping it was Terrance or Blue but instead it was Rodney. He stood at the door with a huge present in his hand. He looked as if he just lost his best friend.

Black- What are you doing here?

Rodney- Please just hear me out. I know I really had no business acting the way I did in the hospital that day but I'm truly sorry. I guess I became jealous. I've never known anyone to be as cool as you at all. Ever since that day at the hospital I haven't been the same and I must confess you got me open, girl. I just want to be your friend, okay?

Black- (giving Rodney a hug) I forgive you. (She released the hug.) Would you like to come in?

Rodney- Of course, and I have something for you. (He walked in the house.)

I closed the door behind him then went and sat on the couch.

Rodney- Here you go. (He handed Black the present.)

Black- Thank you. (She opened the present.)

I began opening the present. I was expecting a blouse or pants but instead it was something even better. It was that dress from the window on 125th Street. My soul uplifted as my heart pounded. I looked at Rodney as he smiled and kissed him so good you would think it was our wedding night. When we released from the kiss I could feel him shake.

Rodney- I detect you like it.

Black- I love it so much. Thank you. Do you have anything to do tonight?

Rodney and I spent that whole night in just talking and watching movies. As always he made me happy and feel good. Though I had several issues he helped me put them to the side. About 2:30 A.M. I received a phone call from Isles and Blue. I didn't want Rodney listening to me so I went upstairs.

Black- What's up?

Blue- A lot is up. First I would like to start with I'm sorry. I know I had no business yelling or getting mad at you. It wasn't your fault.

Black- Well, I'm sorry also. Maybe we should have checked the hotel first. It was my fault.

Isles- No, it's not your fault. It's good we didn't go and get them because where would we go? We have bigger issues than that anyway. Our biggest concern is getting them out of his hands before that Jumble ends.

Black- I have no clue where else he would take them.

Isles- I have an idea but we have to meet Mr. Owens tomorrow. I set up a meeting for tomorrow night at 10:00 P.M. So get some rest; we have a busy day tomorrow.

Black- Okay.

Isles- Have you seen Terrance?

Black- No, he's mad at me still. He's staying at the Byron Hotel.

Isles- I'll go by and talk to him in the morning. I have to get him for the meeting anyway.

Black- I doubt if he wants to talk to me but tell him I have something important to tell him. Okay?

Isles- Yeah, I'll tell him.

Blue- Black, you and I have to talk, okay?

Black- Okay, goodnight.

I hung the phone up and went back downstairs to Rodney. He sat on the couch laughing at a movie. He looked at me as he heard me coming from upstairs. Once I saw he had tears in his eyes from laughing I began to laugh also.

Black- What I miss?

After the movie Rodney and I fell asleep on the couch for the night. The following morning my stomach didn't agree with me. I was starting to get to know the inside of a toilet bowl very well. As Rodney knocked on the door I pretended not to hear him so I flushed the toilet and turned on the cold water in the sink and rinsed my mouth. Once again Rodney knocked on the bathroom door.

Rodney- Are you okay in there?

After I was finished rinsing my mouth out I turned the water off then opened the door. Rodney stood there with his eyebrows lifted.

Black- I'm fine, I just felt real sick. Maybe I need to eat. Come on. (She walked downstairs.)

Rodney took me being sick seriously. He cooked me a wonderful breakfast then he went home. I waited in the house until ten o'clock that night for Blue and Isles to pick me up. I prayed Terrance forgave me and was in the car. When I got in the car I noticed he wasn't in there.

Isles- I went to the hotel and they said a Terrance Watson never checked in at that hotel. I don't know if you thought it was that hotel but it's not.

Black- Are you sure?

Blue- Positive. (She pulled off.)

I became angry along with worried. Why would he not want to be around at a time like this? Was he that mad at me? I could feel a tear forming in my eye so I brushed it away. I had to hold my head. Mr. Owens sat in a chair tapping his nervous feet repeatedly.

Isles- So what do you have planned for Thomas? Death?

Warren- No.

Black- What do you mean no? We have to kill that son of a bitch because he has our children and his uncle.

Blue- You know that, Mr. Owens, look what he did to me. We have to kill that man.

Warren- Oh, we will mentally. We don't need the blood on our hands, though. What I need you all to do is get rid of all your identification. I'm talking about driver's license, birth certificates, social security cards, and bills. You have to get rid of it all. What I'm going to do to Thomas is even worse than death. You just all have to play your part and do exactly what I say.

Terrance was still knocked out as he sat up in a chair with his hands tied behind his back. His head held a bloody lump from which someone hit him. He seemed to be in the basement of their home. He didn't get a chance to see who it was but he had a good idea, though. Samantha opened the door and stood in the door way as she looked at Terrance with his eyes closed. She smiled then walked in and closed the door behind her. God only knew what she was thinking. She walked over to him and punched him so hard in his face he woke up.

Terrance- (waking up mad) You stupid bitch. (He tried to kick Samantha.)

Samantha- (laughing as if she were being tickled) Now, now, Terrance, calm down.

Terrance- You know what, Vanessa? When I get loose I'm going to choke you out, throw you into the wall then kick you in your stomach.

Samantha- Really?

Terrance- I promise.

Just then she ran over and bit him hard on his shoulder for five seconds. Terrance screamed until she let go.

Samantha- I hate you so much. You didn't really think I was going to marry your stupid ass, did you? I can't wait until I kill Black. I might even waste her daughter and make you watch.

Terrance- Yeah, then I'm going to make your children watch you die.

Terrance yelled as she kicked him in his right knee. Samantha loved how she tortured him.

Terrance; Did you kill my mother, you evil hoe?

Samantha- Yes. (She kicked Terrance in his left knee.) I did.

Terrance- (screaming) Why? She had nothing to do with it. You took her life for what reason?

Samantha- I killed her because I was paid to, plus she didn't accept me from day one at the dinner.

Terrance put his head down as he held his tears back. He wanted to kill her so bad and he couldn't even reach her.

Terrance- How could you do this type of bullshit with your children around?

Samantha- Well, after I feed them I'm going to take them to their grandparents. I can't have them here tomorrow when I kill you, now can I? (She walked away.)

184

Meanwhile, I was just finishing up my lasagna when my doorbell rang. I was expecting Isles and Blue because we were having our last cooked meal in America. When I opened the door Rodney stood there with a pitiful look on his face.

Black- What's wrong?

Rodney- She told me she hated me. My own mother disowns me.

Black- Well, do you want to talk?

Rodney- I don't mean to keep bothering you but....

Black- (pulling Rodney in the house) Come in.

We sat down on the couch. I didn't know if this was the truth or a lie so he could come over here. It didn't matter anyway because I wouldn't see him any more after tonight anyway.

Rodney- Whatever you're cooking smells good. Did I intrude?

Black- No, not at all, what's going on?

Just as Rodney was about to speak the doorbell rang so I stood up and walked toward the door.

Black- Hold on, Rodney. Who is it?

Blue- It's me, open up.

Once I recognized the voice was Blue's I opened the door. Isles walked in behind her then closed the door behind himself. They hadn't noticed Rodney on the couch until he cleared his throat. It was as if he wanted them to know that he was there.

Black- Um, I don't know if you remember Rodney, but Rodney, this is Isles and you already know Blue.

Rodney- Hi.

Blue- Hi.

Isles didn't speak. Actually he seemed rather mad and hated the fact he was here. I could see Rodney felt uncomfortable.

Rodney- Am I interrupting something, because I can go home. (He stood up.)

Black- No, you're fine. We're about to eat.

Rodney- I'll set up the table.

Black- That'll be great. Thank you.

He got up and went into the kitchen.

Isles- What's he doing here? I thought you weren't seeing him. You do remember how he acted in the hospital, right?

Black- Well, don't you sound like Terrance?

Isles- You know he's going to flip if he catches him here.

Black- Yeah, well, Terrance hasn't been around in three days. Don't get me started, goddamn it. Tomorrow we'll be in Mexico and I won't know where he is for the rest of my life. I can't come back and find him.

Isles- So what, am I supposed to like him?

Blue- No, but even you know we could use his help. Terrance is not coming back or he would have been showed up. Use your head.

We must have spoken some sense into him because he decided to go along with the idea also. I know it was kind of risky because we hardly knew Rodney but what I did know of him was okay. Isles decided he would ask him after we finished dessert.

Isles- Um, don't you ladies have something to do?

Black- (catching on) Right. (She stood up from the table.) Come on, Blue.

Blue stood up and followed me into the greenhouse in back of our house. I never really knew why Judy loved this greenhouse so much until now. It was so beautiful.

Blue- This greenhouse is beautiful.

Black- Judy started it.

Blue- I know you miss her.

Black- I miss her like crazy.

Blue- Yeah, me too.

Black- I love you just as much as I love her and nothing can come between that. (She gave Blue a hug.)

Blue- I love you too, girl. (She released the hug.)

Black- So tell me, what's so important?

Meanwhile, Rodney and Isles sat at the table and continued to talk.

Rodney- So let me get this right. It's a big meeting called the Jumble and it's where several big bosses get together and gamble and trade people. You want me to help you get your uncle, daughter, and nephew back from a man named Thomas. Then you want to flee to Mexico forever with lots of money?

Isles- Right, see, we can take the money from the Jumble by robbing them before we put those mother fuckers in the ground. Chances are you might and might not make it. It's going to be so many people there and they will try to kill you if they feel you want to hurt their boss. It's their job to make sure he's safe at all times. So what do you say?

Rodney- I'm in. What do I have to do?

Isles- First thing we have to do is get rid of all your identification. I'll help you. Oh, yeah, this rule applies to everyone including male or female. If you contact anyone in America after we leave we'll kill you. Chances are if you're caught, we're caught.

Rodney- You got it. (He shook Isles' hand.)

I was still waiting for Blue to tell me what was so important.

Black- Girl, please tell me and stop stalling.

Blue- Okay, you ready? I'm pregnant and you can't tell Isles because I want to be the one to tell him. I don't know a thing about being a mother but I'll have to learn because I'm keeping it.

Blue picked her head up and looked at me.

Blue- Are you mad at me? You look disappointed.
Black- Wow, that's crazy.
Blue- What's crazy?
Black- It's crazy how the both of us get pregnant around the same time. It's like God wants us to get through this and live our lives.
Blue- Hold on, you're pregnant?
Black- Yeah. (She smiled.)
Blue- (screaming) Oh my God, you too? Thank God I'm not in this by myself. Who's the father?
Black- What do you mean who's the father? Terrance, girl.
Blue- Does Rodney know?
Black- No, and it's none of his business.
Blue- It will be once we cross Mexico. We can't tell them because they're not going to let us help and they need our help.
Black- I know.
Blue- Yeah. Do you think it's wrong we're risking our babies' lives?
Black- We're risking their lives by not doing it. Stop worrying.

Just then Isles and Rodney opened the door to the greenhouse and walked in.

Rodney- You girls okay?
Black- Fine, what's up?
Isles- Well, Rodney took the offer and we're going to his place to get rid of all his identification. We'll be back in three hours.
Blue- Okay.

Rodney and Isles had just arrived in front of his house. Rodney took the mail out his mailbox and ripped it up. They trashed everything in his house then burned the rest of his papers.

Isles- We're about to begin our mission.
Rodney- What am I going to do about my car? If I put it in storage they might trace fingerprints.
Isles- Well, I know Blue and Black is bringing their cars so we won't need one yet. You're going to have to do what I did to mines.
Rodney- What did you do?

Isles drove Rodney to a river site.

You sure you don't want to kiss your car one more time? I mean, I kissed my car and I'm not embarrassed.

Rodney- No, I'm sure.
Isles- Okay.

Isles took the car from out of park and put it in drive. They watched it roll down the hill and into the water. Rodney closed his eyes until he heard it hit the water.

Isles- (laughing) It's all over, man. (He patted Rodney on his back.)
Rodney- Hey, what are we going to do about our houses? I'm pretty sure there's more than a thousand prints all over the house.
Isles- Listen, by the time tomorrow rolls in there won't be a trace of who we are. We're just going to disappear off this earth.

Samantha walked briskly into the room that isolated Terrance from the real world then closed the door. She carried a .38 caliber in her right hand. This was the last thing that he would ever see again in his life. He was weak and tired from all the torture and starvation that she put him through. Samantha walked over toward him and laughed. She knew he hated her more than he could ever imagine. Once she was standing right in front of him she began tapping him in the middle of his forehead with the gun.

> Samantha- Wake up, it's time to die, wake up.
> Terrance- (weak) What?
> Samantha- (smacking blood from Terrance's mouth) I said wake the fuck up! (She looked at her watch.) It's only 2:00 A.M. and I'm going kill you early. I was supposed to wait until 8:30 but I have this fetish to kill you now. (She pointed the gun in Terrance's face.)

Though Terrance was one minute away from being dead he began to laugh directly in her face.

> Samantha- What's so funny?
> Terrance- You really want me to tell you?
> Samantha- Yes, tell me.
> Terrance- You know what? Your problem is you want to be heard but no one will listen to you. Well, that's because you're a nobody. Your body and face look good but your brain's fucked up. Your pussy is not even all that anyway, ask me, I know. Your mother must have dropped you on the ground. (He continued laughing.)
> Samantha- I'm glad you think shit stinks. Hope you think bullets in your head is funny.
> Terrance- (changing the subject) Look, Samantha, before I die I want to feel your smooth hands against my face. I want you to hit me so hard you feel it. That's what I want before I die. Please. You can't argue with that, can you?
> Samantha- (confused) Alright, but let's make this quick. Do me a favor, will you? Tell the devil I said, "Move over, I'm coming soon."
> Terrance- Anything you want, just hit me.

Samantha balled her fist up and held it up. She thought it was a little weird that he wanted her to hit him but oh well, what the hell. She swung her fist forward aiming for his nose but her hand was stopped. She became petrified.

Terrance stood up from the chair, grabbed Samantha by her throat, and increased pressure around it. Samantha eyes lit up as she never saw him in this type of manner before.

Samantha- How'd you get loose?

Terrance gave her an evil grin before he gripped her neck tighter.

Terrance- Remember what I told you I was going to do to you when I get loose?
Samantha- (scared) Yes.

He threw her into the wall and watched as she fell to the floor. When he noticed she tried to get up he ran and kicked her in her stomach, then took the gun from her.

Terrance- (cocking the gun back) You can tell the devil yourself. I got to go and help my baby, Black, kill your fat, sloppy boss. (He shot Samantha twice in her chest.)

He watched as her movement grew stiff and still then took a deep breath. As he hurried toward the door an unbearable pain shot through his wrist and ankles. He had spent all last night pulling and ripping from the rope to free himself. He took off his top shirt and wrapped his right wrist then opened the door. As he walked upstairs in her house he walked through the living room. He continued to walk on until he came about the kitchen. He saw her pocketbook lying on the counter so he ran to it and dumped everything out. Her wallet fell on the floor so he picked it up and went through it. He found some money so he counted it. It was close to five hundred dollars so he put it in his pocket. He hurried for the door until he spotted the refrigerator from the corner of his eyes. His stomach was calling it. He ran to it and opened the door. He grabbed a plastic bag from the bottom of the refrigerator and began stuffing food inside then the he went out the door. Meanwhile, I had woke up at 5:15 in the morning thinking about Terrance. Why did he desert me? Why didn't he come and talk to me so I could let him know I was holding his baby? My back porch had the most beautiful scenery in the world. I thought so anyway. This would be the last time I ever stood on the back porch again. This is where Judy and I would come when we argued to make up. I missed her so much. Suddenly I heard the back door open. I thought it was Rodney but it was Blue instead. I guess her baby was keeping her up.

Black- Baby bothering you?

Blue- No, I'm hungry actually.

Black- Yeah, me too.

Blue- (yawning) So why you not in the kitchen cooking?

Black- You know why.

Blue- You know what? I'm just as upset as you are. The last thing I would expect is for him to bail. He doesn't even know you're pregnant. I don't know why he would just up and disappear.

Black- He was mad as hell at me, though.

Blue- There isn't that amount of mad in the world. I hope Thomas didn't get to him.

Black- Please, don't say that. I hope everything goes fine with this Jumble thing.

Blue- It will, don't worry. I'm going to enjoy killing Pink. I hope she brought her boyfriend.

Black- We won't have enough time to watch each other's backs.

Blue- Enjoy smelling America because this is the last time we'll be here.

Black- (smelling the air) Smells like bullshit. (She laughed.)

Blue- Remember, whatever goes down Isles and I will always have your back. I love you.

Black- I love you, too. (She gave Blue a tight hug.)

As we hugged Rodney and Isles stood at the back door watching us.

Isles- Can we know what's the happy occasion?

Blue- It's a woman's world. (She released the hug.) So mind your business.

Rodney- I was going to make some breakfast. We can't do this on an empty stomach. Besides, we have three hours to meet up with Mr. Owens.

After we ate we decide to watch a movie to kill time. Meanwhile, it was close to seven-thirty and the Jumble was crowded with several big-time bosses. Thomas was setting money aside for a new team to work for him. Pink sat next to him watching him count his money. She had no idea what he was counting it for.

Pink- Hey, Thomas, after today I'm going to fall out dead to the world.
Thomas- (giving Pink a wicked smile) I bet you will.

Terrance sat in a truck with a complete stranger. He had hitched a ride from the highway. Terrance hardly made eye contact with the driver at all. As the driver drove he happened to look down and notice Terrance's bloody wrists.

June- Hi, my name is June, what's yours?

Terrance didn't respond.

June- Do you need help, because you're wrists are bleeding?
Terrance- No, thanks, I'm fine. Really.
June- Well, alright, you going to visit some family members?
Terrance- Yes. Look, excuse me, no offense, but could you drive just a little faster and shut up?
June- Look, there's nothing wrong with being concerned. I just….
Terrance- I'll give you five hundred dollars if you can shut up the whole way there and drive faster.

Terrance didn't have to say anything more because the driver pushed hard on the gas. Meanwhile, Detective Cargo sat at his desk looking at a *Playmate* magazine. He was excited but in a calm manner.

Detective Cargo- (looking at the magazine) Oh, you hot thing, you. Stop teasing me. Oh, yeah, that's what I like. (He turned the page.) Grace, you….

Suddenly his door opened and Darlene walked in with several papers in her hand. She spotted his magazine and gave him a sneaky grin. He put the magazine down as he looked at her embarrassed.

Detective Cargo- Do you know how to knock?
Darlene- Yes, but not right now. I have something important to tell you. (She closed the door behind her.) I have every file you ordered. (She placed them on his desk.)
Detective Cargo- Damn, that's a lot of paperwork.
Darlene- I saved you the trouble. I went through them already and you won't believe this.

The information that Darlene gave Detective Cargo was unbelievable. In fact, it triggered his temper. He drove dangerously to my house looking for me. As the detective pulled up to my house his mouth hit the pavement. He couldn't believe what he was seeing. My house had been knocked down and the workers were stacking the bricks that fell.

Detective Cargo- Hey (getting out of his car), what are you doing? Stop.
Worker- Hey, what's your problem? Are you insane?
Detective Cargo- Do I look insane?
Worker- You don't want me to answer that.
Detective Cargo- (holding up his badge) Get me your supervisor.

After a while the supervisor walked over to Detective Cargo and shook his hand.

Detective Cargo- Are you the supervisor?

Frank- Yes, my name is Frank. May I help you?

Detective Cargo- Why are you knocking down this building?

Frank- Well, it was paid for and it's been in progress for about a week. We have one more to do after this one.

Detective Cargo- When, today?

Frank- Yeah. We did three between two days ago and today.

Detective Cargo- May I see those orders?

Frank- Sure, may I see your badge?

Detective Cargo- Yes, you may. (He pulled out his badge.)

It was two minutes from eight as Isles, Blue, Rodney, and I climbed in Mr. Owens' limo. We had only an hour to go.

Warren- Hello, everyone, and good morning. I hope everyone's okay by what we're doing. (He was holding a bag in his hand.)

Black- I've never been as ready in my life.

Blue- I'm a little nervous.

Warren- You'll be just fine.

Isles- It will, don't worry. (He gave Blue a kiss to calm her.)

Warren- The important thing is to follow the procedure. By the time I'm finished with Thomas he'll wish he were dead. Now in the meantime (pulling out a bottle of scotch), we have one hour to get ready. Have a drink with me.

Terrance handed June the five hundred dollars and got out the truck. He had to hurry.

Terrance- Thank you, sir. I appreciate it.

June- Hey, wait, take this. (She handed Terrance a gun.) It's loaded. Take care of yourself.

Terrance- (taking the gun) Thanks, man. (He closed the truck door.)

Terrance stood back as the man pulled off. Now he had two guns and not even an hour to get to the Jumble. What was he going to do about transportation now that he was back in Manhattan? The cruelest thought possessed his mind. He had no choice but to break into a car and highjack it. Detective Cargo sat at his desk roaming through the paperwork he had gotten from the supervisor. Suddenly he froze. He jumped up and grabbed his jacket from his chair and headed out looking for Darlene. After a while he spotted her talking to some female officers in the break room.

Detective Cargo- Darlene, you look so pretty today, so lovely.

Darlene- No, I brought you the files and that's all I'm going to do.

Detective Cargo- Let me have a word with you. (He pulled Darlene up from the chair.) Listen, I'm on to something so big I can taste it. I can bring this all down under an hour, just help me out, though.

Darlene- Why do I always fall into your trap? What is it?

Detective Cargo- Remember last year when that riot broke out in White Plains?

Darlene- You mean the....

Detective Cargo- (interrupting) Yeah, that one. I need you to look through the computer and find the address.

Darlene- It can take all the way up to an hour to get that address.

Detective Cargo- I know but your reward will be great.

Darlene- Okay.

Detective Cargo- Call me on my cell phone when it comes up.

Darlene- Where you going?

Detective Cargo- White Plains, and don't tell anyone until you call me.

He put his coat on and walked out the door. Terrance was speeding in a 2002 Jaguar. He had no idea who it belonged to; he just needed it. He felt that it was too quiet in the car so he turned up the music and pressed hard on the pedal. After about five minutes Terrance reached my house. When he saw the workers picking up the bricks he began to panic.

Terrance- (thinking to himself) Why are they knocking down your house, Black?

Just then he put the car in reverse and headed to the Jumble. Meanwhile, Mr. Owens and I, along with the others, waited for the clock to strike nine. We only had ten minutes to go and the scotch had me feeling like Zena. I knew I was drunk because my vision was blurry. I really didn't know what to expect of this but if the worse were to happen at least I would go with alcohol in my soul.

Blue- Mr. Owens, what's that bag for? Are you going to beat him with it?
Warren- No, it's just a special present for Thomas. I'm pretty sure when he sees it he will recognize it.
Blue- Well, I'm ready to blow some heads and hearts apart. How about you, Mr. Owens? I'm talking to you.

A couple of seconds later we found ourselves laughing until tears came out our eyes.

Rodney- I like that girl. I feel the same way.
Isles- I'm down with that, too. (He gave Rodney a pound/) You're cool after all.
Warren- Well, ladies and gentlemen, I'm glad you're feeling the way you are but as you all know, it's show time. The only ones that you will have to kill without notice is the two men at the front door because they won't let you in without an invitation.

Detective Cargo had just entered White Plains. He knew it wouldn't be long before Darlene called him with the address, but in the meantime he would just drive around and look for it.

Terrance was two miles from the Jumble as traffic held him up. All the lanes were filled with cars and they had come to a stop. He stood in traffic beeping his horn. We had just pulled up to the front door of the Jumble. As always two men stood at the doorway so that no one could get in. They looked fear and heartless.

Warren- Look, let's do this.

Rodney pushed the door open and fired two shots apiece at the men. The bullets entered their heads then they fell to the ground. We all got out of the limo and ran to the front door. Once everyone was out of the car it pulled off. Isles counted to three then kicked the front door open. As we walked in the Jumble several bosses and their workers emerged with panic. Isles, Blue, Mr. Owens, and I pointed our guns directly in the crowd as they pointed their guns back.

Black- Look, we don't want to kill you so just put your guns down. I'm here to get my daughter, nephew, and uncle, so don't fucking get in our way. I have no problem with you people, I just want my family back. Last option, you all can just get the fuck out and pretend as if you never seen us and live to see another day, or you can die with a passion.

The workers began looking at their bosses to see what they were going to do. One big boss looked at another boss and that boss looked at another boss. The last boss nodded his head and stood up. His workers still had their guns pointed at us but we didn't care.

Boss #3- Okay, but only on one condition.
Black- What's that?
Boss #3- Make sure you hurt that greedy son of a bitch.
Warren- No problem.
Boss #3- Alright, people, let's move and get out of here.

All of the workers and their bosses put their gun down and headed out of the door. When everyone was completely out of the building I closed the door and locked it. Thomas and the others must have heard the gunshots that Rodney fired outside because they ran to the window and looked out. When they looked out they saw the two men lying dead on the ground.

Thomas- Get out! You all have to find somewhere to go and you can't stay in here.

Pink, Red, Yolonda, and Felix all looked at Thomas as if he were crazy.

Red- Well, where are we going to go? We don't even know what's going on.
Thomas- I don't give a shit. Get out.

After a while they got out and watched Thomas close the door then lock it. Pink and Yolonda ran in the same direction while Pink and Felix ran in the opposite direction. Uncle Sam and the children were in the basement of the building scared as they heard the gunshots go off. He pulled the children close to him and held them tight.

Lily- What's going on, Uncle Sam?
Uncle Sam- I don't know, honey, but it's okay.
Warren- Okay, let's get this on the move. Pink you go and find Pink; Isles, you find Felix. Black, you and Rodney go and find Red and Yolonda, and I'll find my buddy. Hurry, we don't have much time.

We all ran off in separate directions of the building. Anyway, Darlene sat at the computer waiting for the address to pop up. Suddenly she heard Lt. Franks calling for her so she ignored him. He continued to walk until he came upon her sitting at the computer.

Lt. Franks- Darlene, do you have a hearing problem? I've been calling you forever. Have you seen Detective Cargo?
Darlene- No, I haven't. I'm busy.
Lt. Franks- Busy, huh? Well, I have a job for you. Come on.

Darlene hesitated but got up eventually because she couldn't risk her job. As soon as she walked out the door with Lt. Franks the address popped up on the screen.

Meanwhile, Pink had split up from Felix and hid in a closet. She was tired of running and scared of what was going to happen. She cocked her gun back then took a deep breath. Her heart pounded like a drum as she turned the knob slowly then peeked out. When she noticed no one was in the room she peeked her head out farther. She looked to her left and no one was there. Just as soon as she went to look to the right Blue struck her so hard in the face that she fell to the floor. Blue then pulled Pink out of the closet by her hair. Pink screamed as she dropped her gun.

> Blue- No pain. No gain. (She kicked the gun away from Pink then kicked Pink in the stomach.)

As Blue went to kick Pink again, Pink pulled her down by her leg and got on top of her. Pink began pounding Blue in her face.

> Pink- (pounding on Blue) Don't you ever, ever act crazy on me again.

Blue took her legs and wrapped them around Pink then threw her backwards onto the floor and kicked her face. Pink grabbed the gun then stood up as Blue got up.

> Pink- What's the matter, Blue? Taking it personal I'm fucking your husband?
> Blue- No, I'm taking it personal; you didn't shoot to kill. Never shoot someone and don't kill.
> Pink- My aim was a little off this time but I guarantee I won't miss this time.

Before Pink could shoot her gun off Blue took out hers and shot Pink in the heart. Pink fell dead to the floor.

Isles ran after Felix, shooting. Every once in a while Felix shot his gun back.

Isles- Why you running, Felix? You have enough heart to hit a woman, hit me.
Felix- Why don't you put that gun down?
Isles- Okay, if you put down your gun I will fight like a man.

Thomas lay against the door he hid behind and took a deep breath. He began to become petrified as he watched someone turn the knob from the outside. He began to look around to find somewhere to hide but there wasn't anywhere to hide. Suddenly he spotted the window and ran to it. He took the lock off it then lifted it up and climbed out the window. As soon as he closed the window back down he could hear two gunshots proceed through the door.

Warren- (kicking the door in) Thomas, are you in here?

Mr. Owens walked in and found nothing so he walked back out. Thomas climbed over to another window and lifted it then climbed in. Red and Yolonda were hiding well, because Rodney and I couldn't find them.

Rodney- Where the hell are they?
Black- I don't know but they can't be too far because this place is only but so big. Keep looking.

Rodney and I walked on. As we came close to this room gunshots were fired from behind us. Rodney and I ducked and took cover, though that left us on two opposite sides of the building. I could still see Rodney. Meanwhile, Isles and Felix stood fighting. They had placed their guns on the floor and Felix had the best of Isles for about five seconds then Isles took the cake. Isles pounded and kicked on Felix's body until it grew weak and tired as he fell on the floor.

Isles- I'm going to make you my bitch. (He reached down for Felix.)

Just as soon as Isles went to reach down for Felix, he kicked Isles in the stomach then face. As Isles fell to the ground in pain, Felix jumped up then grabbed his gun and took off. After Isles got up he grabbed his gun then ran after Felix. He was mad as he walked through the building holding his stomach looking for Felix. As he continued to walk he could hear water running so he followed the sound of the water. Isles walked into a bathroom that encountered a Jacuzzi filling with water. Isles took five steps into the bathroom then heard someone running for him so he turned around.

Felix- (running for Isles) I'm going to kill you!

Isles' reflex caused him to throw Felix in the Jacuzzi filling with water. As Felix landed in it he hit his head on the side of it, which knocked him out cold. Isles became more furious and spotted a radio plugged in on the sink, so he walked over and picked it up then threw it in with Felix. Immediately Felix began to fry. Isles watched with a smile on his face as Felix kicked and screamed to his death. When it was all over Isles walked away laughing. Rodney and I continued to look for Red and Yolonda. After they fired the shots they just disappeared. I prayed Rodney would be okay, drunk and alone. As I began walking down a hallway I stopped because I heard footsteps. Once I stopped I didn't hear them anymore so I continued to walk. As I started walking I could hear the extra footsteps again so once again I stopped. This time I looked behind me and just as I did Red hit me directly in my face. We began fighting immediately.

Red- What's the matter, Black, need a tongue up your ass? (She knocked the gun from Black's hand.)
Black- No... I'm being stuck by the real power. When I'm done with you the only way you'll be able to tongue something is through your imagination. (She knocked the gun from Red's hand.)

Suddenly I heard Yolonda calling for Red.

Yolonda- Red, where are you? Are you okay?

I began to panic because it was impossible for me to handle the both of them with guns. Damn, where the hell was Rodney? Just then Red hit me and I fell to the floor. From the floor I could see Yolonda come in the room pointing her gun directly at me. My heart felt captured.

Red- What took you so long?
Yolonda- Sorry, baby, now stand that bitch up. I'm going to shoot her right in her neck.
Red- Oh, with pleasure, baby. (She pulled me off the floor by my hair then grabbed my shirt.)

I wanted to do something, but what could I do?

Yolonda- This is for the fork you put to my neck.

I just knew my life was over. Then the perfect idea came to me. Just as Yolonda pressed the trigger I pulled Red in the way then I fell to the floor. The bullet entered Red's neck as if it would have done mine. Blood ran helplessly down her neck as she fell to the floor dead.

Yolonda- No... oh, God, what did I do? Red (crying), Red.

Yolonda looked at me with an evil look on her face. She wanted to kill me for doing what I did.

Black- I'll tell your boyfriend (looking at Red on the floor) you said hi.
Yolonda- (crying) Please do. (She pointed the gun at Black.)

I closed my eyes as three gunshots went off. I thought they said death was painful because I sure didn't feel any pain. I opened my eyes and noticed Rodney standing in front of me.

Rodney- Girl, you okay? I was looking for you like crazy.

Black- Yeah, I'm fine. (She looked at Yolonda dead next to Red.) Thanks.

Rodney- (helping Black off the floor) Come on.

Terrance had just parked the car in front of the Jumble then got out his car. When he walked up to the door and saw the two men lying dead on the ground he began to panic. He tried to open the door but it was locked, so he took out his gun and shot the lock off and kicked in the door.

Terrance- Black! Black!

Black- (looking at Rodney) Is that Terrance?

Rodney- I don't know. Is it?

Terrance- Black!

Black- (excited) Oh my God, it is Terrance. Terrance, I up....

Suddenly I was pistol whipped from the back. I fell to the ground as Rodney laughed. Meanwhile, Darlene had just finished up some paperwork for Lt. Franks as she sat down at the computer. She almost forgot about getting the address for Detective Cargo, so she looked at the screen and picked up her phone and called Detective Cargo. The phone rang three times before he picked it up.

Detective Cargo- (answering his phone) Hello?

Darlene- I have that address for you.

Detective Cargo- Great, what is it? (He grabbed a pen and pad from his glove compartment.)

Darlene- First tell me you love me.

Detective Cargo- You know I love you, Darlene. (He smiled.)

Darlene- Okay, it's 493 Vaxen Bridge.

Detective Cargo- Thank you, honey. Now tell Lt. Franks I need major backup. (He hung up his phone.)

Detective Cargo put his sirens on and headed for the Jumble. My head ached as I began to wake from the hit Rodney had given me from behind. As I opened my eyes he was the first and only person I saw. I became confused. My legs and hand were tied behind my back as I sat in a chair.

Black- Rodney, what the hell are you doing? Why did you hit me? Untie me.

Rodney- (looking Black in her eyes) You really are stupid, huh? You just don't get it. I don't like you at all and I only put up with your shit because I was paid to.

Black- What do you mean you were paid to?

Rodney- (walking over to the closet and opening it) I was paid to kill you by…

Rodney looked at the closet as I waited impatiently to see who it was that paid him to kill me. Suddenly Thomas walked out. I could feel my heart pounding as if I were running.

Thomas- I see the plan worked out well.

Meanwhile, Mr. Owens heard the gunshots that proceeded through the door and ran toward the top of the stairs. Just as he reached Terrance was running up the stairs. Mr. Owens pointed the gun directly in Terrance's face before he could even reach the top step. Terrance froze and put his hands up in the air. Isles ran from out a room and spotted Mr. Owens about to kill Terrance.

Isles- Mr. Owens, no, please, don't shoot him, he's good, he's with us.

Warren- I don't remember seeing him at the meeting when we had it.

Isles- I know but he's fine. (He looked at Terrance.) Where the hell have you been? You know we've been looking for you. I thought you bailed on us.

Terrance- Look, it's a long story, where's Black?

Isles- Well, her and Rodney went to look for….

Terrance- Oh, shit, we have to get to her.

Warren- What's wrong?

Terrance- Samantha held me hostage for four days. She tried to kill me. That's not the fucked-up part. Also, Rodney is her husband. He was the one hired to kill her, not Samantha. She was just hired to take me away from Black.

Isles- We have to hurry and get to her.

Terrance ran to find me with Isles and Mr. Owens behind him. Meanwhile, Thomas paced back and forth in front of me. My entire body was shivering with fear. I was upset because everything about Rodney was lie. Everything. He was just a coldhearted hit man who couldn't care less who lived.

Thomas- (looking at Black) You have no idea what you interrupted. You're the one who got in the way of your father's money. My father had intentions of taking all your father's profit but he caught on to what my father was trying to do and he gave everything to you. What you fail to realize is that my father planned your whole life, from start to finish. See, your father was a smart man when it came to his money. I can't argue with that, but what I can tell you is that you're going to give me the codes before you die or I will bring your daughter up here and torture her in front of you until you give them to me. You know, when I saw you girls having problems with the group I offered them a deal they couldn't refuse. Everyone went along with it but Grey.

Black- So you had her and your child killed, right?

Thomas- Oh, I see you've been doing your homework. Well, I paid Samantha to kill her and she did a great job. She just forgot to get that large sum of money I gave Grey. I told Grey that the money was so she can move and get on with her life, when actually it was the money to pay Samantha after she killed her.

Black- You stupid bastard! I'm going to fucking kill you. You didn't have to kill her! You didn't have to kill her! (She was crying.)

Thomas- Yes, I did or her child would have encountered everything I worked for. That shit was not going to happen.

Black- (looking at Rodney) You fucking liar. You're going to die also.

Rodney- Well, maybe if you would have given me some ass I would have killed you sooner. You didn't really think I was going to settle down and have a loving family with you, did you? Oh, shit, you did. I'm sorry to have led you on. I already have a loving wife and children. Dummy, you think I don't see how much you love pretty-boy Terrance. I'm not getting caught up in (being sarcastic) my world of Black's pregnancy. What, you think I didn't see that pregnancy test in the bathroom, duh.

Black- (screaming) I'm going to kill you.

Rodney- Oh, stop it. You're such a bad mommy as well as a dead one. Until next time (cocking his gun back), sweet dreams. (He pointed his gun at Black.)

My time to die had come earlier than what I thought. I closed my eyes and held my breath as three gunshots went off. I heard something hit the floor though it wasn't me. I opened one eye and looked to see what happened. Mr. Owens, Isles, and Terrance had emptied one bullet apiece into Rodney and killed him. Thomas' eyes grew extremely wide as he looked back at them. Still their guns were pointed but this time at him. He dropped his gun immediately.

Mr. Owens- Where are those children?

Thomas- What children?

Mr. Owens- Don't play stupid and tick me off. Tell me now or it's over for you.

Thomas- Okay, they're downstairs in the basement.

At that point Terrance ran over and started to untie me.

Thomas- What are you going to do with me?

207

Just then Mr. Owens walked over and pistol whipped Thomas. He fell to the floor knocked out. Mr. Owens took a gun out of the bag he had been carrying, put it in Thomas' hand then whipped the prints off of the gun. Terrance had just finished taking the rope from my ankles.

Mr. Owens- Now, let's find those kids and get the hell out of here.

We ran downstairs into the basement looking for them. When we got down there, there were several doors so we began calling for them.

Black- Uncle Sam, Lily, Derrick. Where are you?
Blue- Eric, it's your mommy, where are you? Oh, God, where are they?
Terrance- Uncle Sam...

Just as Terrance called for Uncle Sam he answered back.

Uncle Sam- (banging on the door) We're in here.

Terrance ran to the door where they were.

Terrance- Stand back, I have to shoot through the door.

Uncle Sam grabbed Lily and Derrick then ran to the other side of the room.

Uncle Sam- Cover your ears, guys.

Lily and Derrick did so.

Uncle Sam- Go ahead.

Terrance shot four times through the door then kicked it in. We were happy to see that everyone was okay.

Lily- Mommy! (She ran to Black.)

Black- Are you okay, honey?

Lily- Yeah.

Blue- (looking at Derrick) Hi, Derrick, are you okay?

Derrick- I'm fine. Could you take me out of here, please?

Isles- Sure, just grab my hand and don't let go.

Terrance- (grabbing Lily's hand) Same thing goes for you, don't let go.

We all ran. We had to get out before that detective arrived. We were upstairs and the front door was in sight. All we had to do was run down the stairs. As we were going down the stairs to get out the door Detective Cargo jumped in front of us at the door.

Detective Cargo- Where do you think you're going?

I felt stupid because all the hard work we just put into getting these kids and my uncle back we failed right before the door. We were going to jail for life and I couldn't deal with that. I could feel tears pushing through so I let them out.

Black- Fuck.

Detective Cargo- I know everything that happened. Girl (looking at Black), I've never had any female play as smart as you. I know several convicts that couldn't compare with you. I know what you've been through starting from your family being murdered to this. I also know that it's not your fault. The only thing is the State won't care what you've been through. I do, though. Today you caught me in a good mood because the person I want the most is upstairs, right?

Black- (crying) Right.

Detective Cargo- Did you kill him?

Black- No.

Detective Cargo- Good, because he's going to suffer for all the people he and his father killed. Including my father. You don't know it but you helped me out a lot. The only thing I can do is to repay you.... You have to hurry up and get out of here before my boss and backup arrives, but I'll tell you one thing. If I catch you, your friends, or these children one toe back across the border I'll put every last one of you under the jail. You understand?

Black- (wiping her tears away) Hell yeah. Shit, this is the last time you'll ever see what our asses look like. Let's go. (She ran to the limo.)

I couldn't believe what had happened as we all ran for the limo. As we were pulling off I looked back at the detective. He wasn't a bad person after all. When we were out of sight Detective Cargo took his handkerchief out of his pocket and wiped down the car that Terrance stole. He finished just in time before Lt. Franks arrived. He had so many police cars behind him you'd think it was some type of hostage situation. The policemen jumped out the car.

Detective Cargo- Check inside the house.

The policemen ran inside the house with their guns up as other policemen checked to see if the two men Rodney killed had pulses. Meanwhile, Thomas began to move slowly as he woke up from being hit on the head. He had no idea what he was in for. He opened his eyes, though his sight was still blurry. Once he heard the footsteps coming upstairs he clamped the gun that was in his hand. As one of the officers entered the room he spotted Thomas on the floor with the gun.

Officer- Freeze, don't move. Put the weapon down and put your hands up.

Thomas looked at the gun that was in his hand then dropped it. He had no idea where that gun had come from. Little did he realize that gun killed more than forty people within twelve years, including Grey and Detective Cargo's father. Me and Blue's cars was already parked at the airport so that's where we headed to catch our flight. Once we got to Mexico I gave Mr. Owens his diamonds back plus interest as I promised him then we went our separate ways. Blue and I decided to tell Isles and Terrance the good news on the plane. They were a little angry we risked our unborn children's lives, but they were even happier we made it out alive. Uncle Sam decided he would live with us because he wanted to be around for the children while Thomas suffered the electric chair.